Kids
WHO
KILL

Herma Silverstein

Twenty-First Century Books
Brookfield, Connecticut

Twenty-First Century Books
A Division of
The Millbrook Press
2 Old New Milford Road
Brookfield, Connecticut 06804

Library of Congress Cataloging-in-Publication Data
Silverstein, Herma.
Kids who kill / Herma Silverstein.
p. cm.
Includes bibliographical references and index.
Summary: Examines the causes, cases, and social and
personal impact of the increasing incidence of murders
being committed by children and teenagers.
1. Juvenile homicide—Juvenile literature. [1. Murder.] I. Title.
HV9067.H6S58   1997   97-8706
364.15'23'083—dc21   CIP
                                                            AC
ISBN 0-8050-4369-1

Printed in the United States of America

5   7   9   10   8   6   4

Photo Credits
pp. 4, 43, 56: © AP/Wide World Photos; p. 24: © Abarno/The Stock Market;
p. 30: Anthony Nagelmann/FPG International; p. 46: © Dennie Cody/FPG
International; p. 65: © Gilles Mingasson/Gamma Liaison; p. 94: © Kevin
Horan; p. 110: © Mark Richards; p. 114: © Lester Sloan/Gamma Liaison.

CONTENTS

Janie Fields, grandmother of Robert Sandifer, and other
family members and friends gather by his coffin at funeral services
on September 7, 1994. He was eleven years old when he died.

ONE

WHO ARE THE KIDS WHO KILL?

ON A SUNNY SEPTEMBER afternoon in 1994, mothers from the Roseland community of Chicago's South Side took their kids to church. They were not going to Sunday services. Rather, they were taking their kids to see eleven-year-old Robert Sandifer lying dead in his coffin. The mothers hoped the experience would put enough fear in their kids to keep them safe.

Nicknamed "Yummy" for his love of cookies, Robert lay dressed in a suit way too big for his young body, surrounded by his stuffed animals. Kids looking at him could still see the stitches on his face, where bullets fired into the back of his head had torn through his flesh.

How did Yummy end up dead at eleven years old? Much of the answer lies in the fact that the only photograph his family could find for the funeral program was his mug shot. For most of his short life, Yummy was a criminal. To understand why Yummy was busy learning how to hot-wire cars and shoot guns when most fifth graders are busy learning math and science, it is necessary to understand what his life was like. Yummy's mother, Lorina, had her first child at age fifteen. Then, in rapid succession, she had seven more. She left Yummy's abusive father, dropped out of tenth grade, and went on welfare, not to support her children but to pay for her crack habit.

Lorina was first charged with child neglect in 1984, when she failed to follow doctors' orders for treating her two-year-old son's eye infection. Yummy's older brother eventually went blind. The next year, when Yummy was only twenty-two months old, he was rushed to the hospital, covered with scratches on his neck and bruises on his arms and chest. Lorina was put on probation by the Department of Children and Family Services (DCFS). A year later, police found Yummy with long welts on his legs from being beaten with an electric cord, and second-degree burns on his shoulders and buttocks caused by cigarettes being held to his skin. Police removed the children from the home.

Now Yummy's life consisted of being shuttled between foster homes, detention centers, and his gang's safe houses. The police arrested him again and again. But the most they could do under Illinois law was put him on probation. Cook County Public Guardian Patrick Murphy said, "If ever there was a case where the kid's future was predictable, it was this case. What you've got here is a kid who was made and turned into a sociopath by the time he was three years old."[1]

When a psychiatrist asked Yummy to complete the sentence "I am very . . . ," the word he chose was *sick*.[2] Here was a lonely child full of self-hate and mistrust. In 1986, Yummy and his siblings were placed with his grandmother Janie Fields. Neighbors said the whole family—ten aunts and uncles and thirty grandchildren all living together— was noisy and dirty.

THE TWO SIDES OF YUMMY

People who knew Yummy said he could be two different little boys. On the one hand, he was a fierce fighter who would take on big kids and beat them up. "Yummy would ask you for 50¢, and if he knew you were scared and you gave him the money, he'd ask for another 50¢," says Steve Nelson, age eleven. He was a bully who broke into his school and stole money. When he wasn't stealing cars, he was throwing things at them or setting them on fire.[3]

But Yummy had a sweet side, too. Lulu Washington, who sells discount candy out of her house, says, "He just wanted love. And for love, he could be kind. He'd say thank you, excuse me, pardon me." He loved animals and basketball and had a way with bicycles. He once merged two bikes into a single working tandem.[4]

The odds of Yummy's reaching age twelve dropped considerably when he joined the Black Disciples gang, whose leaders use kids as drug runners and hit men because they are too young to be seriously punished if caught. They are also not likely to live long. "If you make it to nineteen around here, you are a senior citizen," says Terrance Green, himself nineteen.[5] Before he was murdered, Yummy committed twenty-three felonies. He was convicted twice and given probation, the state's stiffest penalty for a child his age.

In the fall of 1993, Yummy was placed with the Lawrence Hall Youth Services, which runs homes for troubled teens. He ran away to his grandmother. In July, he went on a church trip to Six Flags Great America, an hour out of Chicago. He was too small to get on most of the rides. But Yummy was not too small to kill. A month later, he shot and killed fourteen-year-old Shavon Dean.

Shavon lived around the corner from Yummy. Her

mother said, "I used to carry him as a young boy to church. He sang in the choir with my daughter. He was a baby, just like my daughter was a baby."[6] On a Sunday night in August, her family was preparing a family barbecue. Shavon left to walk a friend home. She never made it back. Yummy, sent by his gang on a mission of revenge sparked by a drug feud with a rival gang, opened fire with a 9mm semiautomatic into a crowd of kids playing football. Shavon was struck in the head and died within minutes.

For the next three days, as police stormed the neighborhood, gang members shuttled Yummy between safe houses. He appeared on a neighbor's porch, frightened, asking the neighbor to call his grandmother so he could turn himself in. The woman went to phone, but when she returned, Yummy was gone. The police can only guess what happened next. Fearing Yummy would crumble under police pressure if arrested, Derrick Hardaway, fourteen, and his brother Cragg, sixteen, fellow gang members, found Yummy. They promised to drive him out of town. Instead, they drove him to a dark railroad underpass and shot him execution-style. His body was found lying facedown in the mud with two .22-caliber bullet holes in the back of his head.

People who saw the child in Yummy, not the killer, miss him. "Everyone thinks he was a bad person," says Kenyata Jones, twelve. "But he respected my mom, who's got cancer. Yummy used to come over for sleep-overs. We'd bake cookies and brownies and rent movies. . . . He was my friend, you know? I just cried and cried at school when I heard about what happened. And I'm gonna cry some more today, and I'm gonna cry some more tomorrow too."[7]

•   •   •

Sadly, what happened to Yummy Sandifer is not an unusual event. Kids are committing murder at an alarming rate—in drive-by gang shootings, in schools, and in families. For thousands of children, violence has become a daily part of life. In many neighborhoods, random gunfire by teen gangs makes kids who are not gang members afraid to play outside. Every day, in schools across the country, body searches for concealed weapons come before roll call.

According to the U.S. Department of Justice, every day in the United States, ten kids age sixteen and under are killed by handguns. And increasingly, kids are the ones pulling the triggers.[8] Murders committed by kids under age eighteen tripled between 1984 and 1994. If statistics remain the same, juvenile homicides will increase by 25 percent by the year 2005.[9] Homicide is now the leading killer of black males age fifteen to twenty-four, and the second leading cause of death for white youths. (Car accidents are the first.)[10]

Every day, the nation's newspapers carry stories such as the case of two sixteen-year-old Florida boys who murdered a Dutch woman tourist who mistakenly went into a rough Miami neighborhood; or that of a young mother who fell to her death under a New York subway train when a fifteen-year-old boy tried to steal her $60 earnings.[11]

No matter where we live, the rising number of kid killers should concern us all. There are currently 39 million children under age ten in the United States. Therefore, by the twenty-first century, the number of kids fifteen to nineteen, the ages at which most kids commit violent crime, will be booming. "This is the calm before the crime storm," says James Alan Fox, dean of the college of criminal justice at Northeastern University in Boston, Massachusetts.[12] "This generation of youth . . . is more violent than any before it. . . . Far more of today's young people have weapons, and they are willing to pull the trigger over trivial matters."[13]

If something is not done to stop kids from killing, by the year 2000 juvenile homicide will more than likely have touched the lives of everyone in the United States. As with the AIDS virus, it is possible either you or someone in your family will have been directly affected by a juvenile homicide, or you will know someone whose life has been so affected.

In addition, as the number of violent offenders increases, many more deeply troubled adolescents will be entering the already overcrowded juvenile courts. Juvenile lockup facilities are filled to the maximum, and most cities have no plans to build more. So where will these new kid killers go? Crime consultant Donna Hamparian of Columbus, Ohio, says even if more youths are put behind bars, the projected violator totals are so high that "we can't build enough prisons to keep all of them locked up."[14]

To make room for more juvenile offenders coming into the system, overcrowded facilities simply give many offenders early parole. Probation officers have more kids to oversee than they can handle, so these kids are not watched closely to make sure they obey the terms of their parole. The kids end up back on the streets, committing more crimes, including murder. In New York City's Family Court, more than 90 percent of juvenile cases are *felonies* (crimes such as murder, rape, and assault, for which punishment is death or imprisonment for one year or more).[15]

"We've got an epidemic of youth violence," says Deborah Prothrow-Stith, M.D., assistant dean of government and community programs at Harvard's School of Public Health, in Boston.[16] These figures are actually lower than the real instances of murders committed by kids, as many children who kill are not arrested. Rather, they are dealt with in a less severe legal fashion, such as putting them in foster homes or on probation in the custody of parents. In fact, most state laws say juveniles under age seven are not responsible for their criminal acts, including homicide.

WHAT IS JUVENILE CRIME?

Juvenile crime is any act committed by a minor (anyone under eighteen) that would be considered a crime if committed by an adult, such as vandalism, burglary, assault, or murder. Less serious juvenile crimes, such as truancy (skipping school) and running away from home, are called *status offenses.* Kids who commit illegal acts are called *juvenile offenders,* or more popularly, *juvenile delinquents.* Kids who commit crimes are usually sent to juvenile court. However, kids who commit felonies may be tried in adult criminal court and be given adult prison sentences.

Because of the rising number of juvenile homicides, people involved in law enforcement are pushing to change the long-held belief that kids who kill should be treated differently from adult murderers. For example, in Massachusetts, kids as young as fourteen are being tried as adults; Oregon has lowered its minimum age from fourteen to twelve; Wisconsin tries kids age ten as adults; and Tennessee has eliminated *any* minimum age for trying kids as adults.[17]

KINDS OF MURDERS COMMITTED BY KIDS

The kinds of murders committed by kids are the same as those committed by adults. Some are unpremeditated crimes of passion, such as those committed in the course of date abuse or jealous rage over a boyfriend or girlfriend. Other murders may be a response to sexual or physical abuse by parents, siblings, relatives, or dating partners.

Still others are premeditated, motivated by greed, lust, and revenge. And some kids kill for no reason at all. In these so-called thrill killings, kids pick someone to murder at random merely for the thrill of committing murder. In addition, many kids who kill are gang members who murder because of turf wars or as part of initiation rites or drug deals. Regardless of the kind of murder, most teen homicides are committed by kids high on drugs or alcohol.

PROFILE OF KIDS WHO KILL

Who are the kids who kill? The majority are boys. And of these boys, the majority are African-Americans ages fourteen to seventeen. Part of the reason for this statistic is that African-American males greatly outnumber white, Latino, or Asian males in this age group. And these boys are much more likely to face problems linked to crime, such as poverty, family breakdowns, and poor education. Therefore, they are disproportionately involved in crime. Sixty-one percent of juveniles arrested for murder in 1994 were African-American.[18]

Boys of any race who kill tend to be emotionally cold and impulsive. They lack empathy (the ability to feel what another is feeling) for their victims. Kathleen Heide, a Florida psychotherapist, gives the example of a teen who gunned down and paralyzed a jogger who refused to give him a gold neck chain. Asked what a better outcome might have been, the boy said, "He could have given me his rope [chain]. I asked him twice."[19] Carol Kelly, a Chicago juvenile court judge, describes the case of two boys, ages ten and eleven, who lured a five-year-old to the top floor of a housing project and pushed him out the window. Neither boy ever expressed any remorse for the death of their victim.[20]

Girls of any age are extremely unlikely to kill. When they do, girls rarely kill strangers. Instead, they usually kill abusive family members. Sometimes girls kill in the course of committing another crime, such as robbery. In these cases, girls rarely act alone, usually having a female accomplice.

Although more juvenile boys than girls commit murder, the profile for both boys and girls who kill is the same: most come from single-parent families, or families broken by divorce, in which one or both parents are alcoholics, mentally disturbed, neglectful, or abusive. Many of these kids have spent time in foster care. Most of them are left on their own after school while their parent or parents are at work, with no adult to supervise them and with no after-school activity to occupy them until their parents return. In addition, these kids usually have low verbal IQs and poor grades and do not have many friends.

Kids who kill are also more likely to experiment with drugs and alcohol at an early age, are impulsive, and get into trouble with the law by an early age, sometimes by the third grade. In the majority of cases, either one or both of their parents have committed criminal acts. In fact, more than half of all kids in long-term juvenile institutions in the United States have immediate relatives who have been incarcerated.[21]

CHILD ABUSE, AND KIDS WHO KILL

For many of these kids, committing murder is the end of a journey that began when they were victims of abuse themselves. From 1980 to 1992, reports of abused and neglected children almost tripled, from 1 million to 2.9 million.[22] Practically since they were infants, these kids have watched their parents act violent when upset or angry. Thus, these kids learned from their parents that violence is the way to express anger, frustration, and disappointment.

According to a 1995 report by the Center for Juvenile Justice in Pittsburgh, Pennsylvania, the single most consistent characteristic of juvenile homicides is that kids who kill usually have witnessed, or have been directly victimized by, domestic violence.[23] And the most common form of domestic violence witnessed by juveniles who kill is spousal abuse (one parent assaulting the other). Children exposed to family violence commit more than twice as many crimes as those from nonviolent families. A 1988 study of fourteen juveniles on death row by New York University psychiatrist Dr. Dorothy Otnow Lewis found that twelve had been victims of brutal physical abuse and five had been sodomized by relatives.[24]

BRAIN DAMAGE, AND KIDS WHO KILL

Dr. Lewis's death row study also found proof for the theory that there is an association between brain damage and juvenile homicide. All fourteen death row juveniles had symptoms consistent with brain damage. Eight had experienced head injuries severe enough to result in hospitalization, and nine had serious neurological abnormalities, including abnormal reflexes, seizure disorders, and abnormal EEGs (brain-wave findings).[25]

This study also found that most kids who kill have learning difficulties thought to result from brain damage and have experienced academic problems prior to killing. For example, ten of the fourteen juveniles had major learning problems, only three were reading at grade level, and three had never learned to read. Only two had IQs in the normal range.

PSYCHOLOGICAL DISTURBANCES, AND KIDS WHO KILL

Many kids who kill are psychologically disturbed. Antisocial behavior, such as fighting, starting fires, cruelty to animals, or self-mutilation, is a sign of a troubled child. The most frequent diagnosis for these children is "conduct-disordered." The American Psychiatric Association's *Diagnostic & Statistical Manual of Mental Disorders*, used by doctors to diagnose mental illness, found that 6 to 16 percent of males and 2 to 9 percent of females under age eighteen exhibit conduct disorders.[26]

Thirteen-year-old Eric Smith, who murdered Derrick Robie, a four-year-old boy (discussed in Chapter Four), had a history of mentally disturbed acts. In 1989, he strangled a neighbor's cat with a garden hose. Two years later, after a schoolmate died in a car accident, he called the boy's family several times, asking to speak with him. When he had a heated argument with his sister, Stacy, he told his stepfather, "I need help. I feel like I want to hurt somebody."[27] His stepfather suggested he might feel better if he hit something like a stuffed bag. Eric returned later with bloodied knuckles; he had beaten his fists on a tree.

A small percentage of mentally disturbed kids who kill are diagnosed as truly psychotic, meaning they suffer from hallucinations, delusions, thought disorders, or grossly bizarre behavior. In the early morning light, a husky teenage boy sits by the river drinking beer and staring into space. Lying next to him is the nude, bruised body of a teenage girl. So begins the 1987 movie *River's Edge*. The movie is the true story of Anthony Broussard, a sixteen-year-old California boy who raped and strangled his fourteen-year-old girlfriend, dumped her body near a river, then laughed and told friends, "I raped and murdered this chick."[28]

Anthony then took several of his teenage friends to look at the body and throw rocks at it. Finally, after two days, his friends reported the murder to the police. Charged with murder, Anthony was given a psychiatric examination and diagnosed as a chronic paranoid schizophrenic with organic brain disease caused by drug abuse. The psychiatrist testified that Anthony had been devastated when, at age eight, he came home one day and found his mother dead. Afterwards, he stopped maturing, lost all feelings and emotions, and developed a pathological fantasy life. Despite the psychiatrist's diagnosis, Anthony pleaded guilty to the murder and was sentenced to twenty-five years in prison.[29]

GUNS, AND KIDS WHO KILL

Another characteristic of kids who kill is that they own or have access to guns. The Justice Department's *Juvenile Justice Report* found that 80 percent of juvenile homicides are committed with a gun, and those gun homicides increased five times between 1984 and 1993.[30] "This report is a road map to the next generation of crime—unless we do something now," said Attorney General Janet Reno.[31] If her predictions come true, in the twenty-first century we can expect more murders like those that occurred in one week in California during 1995:

Four kids, ages fifteen and sixteen, were arrested in Lake Tahoe for the "thrill shooting" of a fifty-nine-year-old man. Two girls, ages thirteen and fifteen, were charged with beating a thirty-two-year-old woman to death in West Hollywood, then stealing her purse and Mercedes. Five Tustin youths, ages fifteen to seventeen, were charged with slaying a fourteen-year-old boy when he tried to stop them from stealing the stereo system his grandfather had given him.[32]

And increases in homicides by kids are not limited to California. Consider these cases:

Kyle Dylan Moran, sixteen, Michael Shawn Dupuis, fifteen, and Floyd LaFountain, sixteen, of Tampa, Florida, were charged with murdering a seventy-three-year-old man during a burglary. Manuel Sanchez and John Duncan, both twelve, were charged with murdering a migrant worker in Wenatchee, Washington, after he threw rocks at them for firing guns close to him.[33] Michael Est, fourteen, of St. Louis, Missouri, was charged with murdering his father after he complained Michael was playing music too loud, and fifteen-year-old Marcus Currie of Tulsa, Oklahoma, and a seventeen-year-old friend were charged with murdering a mother carrying her baby in a hospital parking lot when she resisted their attempts to steal her purse.[34]

GANGS, AND KIDS WHO KILL

Many killings by juveniles are committed by gangs. On October 28, 1995, Antonio Izquierdo and his eleven-year-old daughter were sitting in a hammock on the front porch of their Huntington Park, California, home. Suddenly three young males in a dark car drove by. Erika's older brother, Alex, thought the boys were arriving for a Halloween party in the backyard, even though it had been canceled earlier. But then the boys opened fire with a rifle. Erika's father tried to shield her from the barrage of bullets. But it was too late. Erika Izquierdo had been shot in the head. She died two hours later. Inches away were two of her friends, Luis Lopez, fifteen, and Adrian Garcia, fourteen. Luis was shot three times, and Adrian five times. Both boys survived their wounds.[35]

In the inner cities, guns, gangs, and drugs have made killing a career path for kids. Children involved in the drug trade get guns to defend themselves against older kids who want their money. The streets offer rent-a-guns for $20 an hour. Gunfire has become so common in classrooms that many schools are banning book bags and tearing out lockers to eliminate hiding places for guns.[36]

THE VENTURA LOCKUP

California has almost ten thousand kids behind bars, more than any other state in the country. The Ventura School outside Los Angeles is one of the state's seventeen juvenile prisons. The facility houses five hundred males and three hundred females, ages fifteen to twenty-four, who have been convicted of serious crimes. These kids serve anywhere from a few months to a few years before being transferred to adult prisons or released on parole.

These kids' stories offer some insights into who the kids who kill are.

One boy said, "I robbed a money carrier, and a police officer chased me, and I killed him. I was fourteen."[37] This boy came from a broken family. He was left alone from the time school let out until late at night, when his mother arrived home from work. Bored, with no after-school activities to occupy his time, he started committing small crimes such as shoplifting or stealing a bike. Then his crimes grew to stealing cars and robbing convenience stores. Until he murdered the police officer, he had never gotten caught. He wonders if he would be in the Ventura Lockup today if he had been caught for the lesser crimes.

Another boy said his criminal career started at age eleven when his parents got divorced. He was filled with anger. "Everything fell apart, because I thought we had the perfect family. But when they got divorced, it was like somebody dropped a bomb."[38] This boy was in a bad mood one day when a stranger said something to him. He does not even remember what the person said. All he remembers is feeling so angry he had to unleash it. He beat the stranger to death with a piece of wood.

A teenage girl in the Ventura Lockup, who was molested from age three until twelve, told this story: "I started drinking when I was eight. I was a full-grown alcoholic by the time I was nine. I got involved with a gang. One day we killed a rival gang member, and I was convicted of murder." About the gun used in the murder, she said, "Getting a gun is as easy as getting a loaf of bread. You can get guns on the street for $20. That's nothing."[39]

Kids who kill come from all races and economic classes. Eric Smith came from a middle-class family and had no previous crime record. On the other hand, eleven-year-old Yummy Sandifer came from a poor family living in Chicago's overpopulated, crime-ridden South Side. He had a rap sheet longer than most adult criminals.[40] Maybe time will heal Shavon's family's grief, but time will never answer one question—why?

TWO

WHY KIDS KILL

ON AUGUST 13, 1990, Anthony Knighton, sixteen, was on his way to the corner market in Deerfield Beach, Florida, to buy cigarettes when he realized he had only 20¢. The market sold cigarettes two for a quarter. He spotted a neighbor, pregnant thirteen-year-old Schanell Sorrells, and demanded she give him a nickel. When she refused, Anthony stuck a .22-caliber revolver against her stomach and pulled the trigger, killing her baby and seriously wounding Schanell. She staggered to the room she shared with her mother and four siblings and fell on a bed. Knighton, who had followed her inside, took a nickel from her room, strolled to the store, and bought two Kools.[1]

• • •

What is it that turns kids like Anthony Knighton into killers? There is no one answer. "Kids are not born bad, they're made bad," says Frances Storr, Ph.D., dean of academic programs at the Erikson Institute for Advanced Study in Child Development in Chicago.[2] In Anthony's case, hurting others was a lesson he learned at an early age. His father beat him constantly until he was three, when his mother died. His next life lessons were neglect and rejection. He was shuttled from relative to relative in Georgia and Florida. By the time he was fifteen, he had moved thirty times. "It seemed like nobody cared about me," he said, "so I guessed I had to do for myself."[3]

Psychologists say children who are passed around like Anthony was have a hard time developing a sense of identity or stability. A child who does not know where he is going to live from one month to the next becomes focused on his immediate needs—like cigarettes—no matter what it takes to get them, even murder. Anthony never had a chance of being rescued from a life of crime. By sixth grade, he had attended seven schools. He was never in one school long enough for anyone to get close to him and counsel him.

When Anthony was fourteen, he was again living with his father. He began selling crack cocaine, eventually developing a $1,000-a-day drug operation. As he made more money, he became a target of other drug dealers. So he borrowed a gun from a friend. By the time he was arrested for murdering Schanell's baby, he owned an arsenal, including a baby Uzi. "A gun in the hands of a fourteen-year-old is much more dangerous than in the hands of a forty-one-year old," says crime expert James Fox. "He has little investment in his life, and he doesn't know the meaning of death."[4]

At sixteen, Anthony had been in juvenile custody nineteen times, charged with such crimes as aggravated assault, auto theft, and drug possession. He was sent to the Better Outlook Center, a halfway house for juvenile offenders in Miami. For the first time in his life, he had a sense of stability and he flourished. When he was released, however, there was no one on the outside to care about him, and eventually he was back to committing crimes—this time, murdering the baby of thirteen-year-old Schanell. Anthony pleaded guilty to third-degree murder and was sentenced to four years in the Indian River Correctional Institution, a medium-security juvenile facility in Vero Beach, Florida. At the time of his parole, two years later, he had no idea where his father and siblings now lived.[5]

WHAT TURNS A KID INTO A KILLER?

Most experts in juvenile homicide agree that much juvenile violence reflects a breakdown of families, especially the absence of fathers in the home, which deprives kids of a key caretaker, role model, and disciplinarian. "The single most reliable predictor of violent crime in a neighborhood is the proportion of single-parent families," says Paul J. McNulty, counsel for the House Judiciary Subcommittee on crime.[6] He says as the number of fatherless households has risen, so has the juvenile crime rate.

Other experts point to the drug trade, which has resulted in the arming of inner-city youth. Crack cocaine arrived in most cities in the mid-1980s, and with it an increase in the murder rate. As arrests and murders eliminated many adult drug sellers, drug dealers started recruiting kids as their new sellers. Domestic violence, child abuse, lower income levels, and a decline in moral values also go into making kids who kill. Other experts blame the media, which feed kids a steady diet of glorified violence. The above reasons, combined with increasing high school dropout rates, drug use, and easy access to guns, make a fertile field for kids who kill.[7]

Many homicides occur while kids are in the middle of committing other crimes. For example, suppose a kid armed with a gun is robbing a house and suddenly the homeowner comes home. The kid panics and shoots the homeowner. Or a kid attempting to mug someone ends up killing the person when the victim fights back. Or a boy who rapes a girl kills her to avoid being identified.

Youth violence is also becoming more widespread and vicious. Three or four decades ago, police worried about juvenile delinquents who stole cars or robbed stores. Today police worry about kids who, armed with guns, not only steal but also kill the car owner or store clerk. And whereas juvenile delinquents of the 1950s sold stolen hubcaps for money, today they sell drugs. Experts on juvenile behavior say what is most frightening is that so many kids who kill show no remorse. Kids are killing for kicks and bragging about it.

LACK OF PARENTAL NURTURING

Many low-income parents are unable to focus on developing a nurturing relationship with their children because they must concentrate on having the rent money on time. When both parents must work two or more jobs, as is often the situation in low-income families, their children are usually left without adult supervision after school. Lack of adult supervision has been shown to be a key factor when kids get into trouble.

Because these kids do not get nurturing from their parents, they turn to other people for love and attention—even if it is the kind of love and attention that leads to killing. These kids usually turn to gang members, who reward them with praise when they steal and deal drugs.

DRUGS, AND KIDS WHO KILL

Still other kids use drugs as a substitute for the natural high they would be getting from nurturing parents. Today, drugs are easily available, and if a kid has the money, buying drugs is not hard to do. Many murders are committed by kids who are high on drugs. Often they are buying or selling drugs or robbing to get money for drugs. One study of juvenile killers found that nearly 73 percent were intoxicated on alcohol or drugs at the time they killed.[8] For kids living in poor, violence-ridden neighborhoods, crime is a way to make money; and money is a way out of poverty. The large sums of money they can make selling drugs lures kids into gangs, who control the drug market in their neighborhoods.

Children who live in more privileged areas also commit murder. "It used to be that you expected crime in some places, and in other places you felt safe. Now it's similar everywhere," says Peter Greenwood, a member of Califor-

Illegal-drug use among high school students declined in the 1980s but is on the rise again in the 1990s. Here a teen buys drugs near his school.

nia's Juvenile Justice Task Force. "It's increasingly clear that everyone's kids are at risk, not just the kids in South-Central."[9] Studies suggest that often these children engage in criminal behavior because they were not punished for previous minor delinquent acts, such as cutting school, shoplifting, or vandalism. And drug abuse is just as big a problem in affluent neighborhoods as in the ghettos. The only difference may be that kids from upper-income families do not have to rob convenience stores to get money for drugs. They just rob their parents' wallets.

THE SEEDS OF VIOLENCE

The seeds of violence in children can be planted even before they are born. A pregnant woman passes on whatever she takes into her body directly to her unborn baby. Therefore, pregnant women who use drugs or alcohol are literally giving their unborn babies a diet of these drugs.

For example, today one in ten babies—some 350,000 babies a year in the United States—has been exposed to cocaine in the womb. Popularly called "crack babies," these infants born to mothers addicted to crack cocaine suffer excruciating withdrawal pains, as outside the uterus they no longer get the drugs the mother was taking. These infants cry and shake uncontrollably, they refuse to take food, and many die. And those who survive are far more likely to have birth defects and learning disabilities. Later, these babies suffer abnormalities in behavior, such as impulsiveness, distractibility, and aggressive behavior.[10]

The crack baby epidemic reached such high proportions in 1988 that thirteen states required doctors to report drug use in pregnancy or positive drug tests in newborns. Nine states consider drug use during pregnancy as child abuse or neglect, and their child welfare systems respond with actions ranging from drug rehabilitation for the mother to placing the child in a foster home. Studies have shown that pregnant mothers who abuse drugs and kick the habit relapse at least once after delivering their babies, and 60 percent continue using drugs. Thus, their children grow up in an environment of drug use and learn that taking drugs is acceptable and part of everyday life.[11]

Babies born to mothers who drink excessive amounts of alcohol while pregnant may be born with what is called *fetal alcohol syndrome (fas)*. Because they have been fed a diet of drugs for nine months in the womb, such babies have a high tendency to abuse drugs and alcohol later in life. In addition, fas babies have lower birth weights and are often born with learning disabilities or other forms of mental retardation, which set them up for failure in school. This failure often leads to extreme frustration, which in turn leads to violent behavior, including murder, because violent behavior is the only activity at which they are successful.[12]

BIOCHEMICAL CAUSES OF VIOLENCE

Today, criminologists are also looking at biochemical imbalances in the brain as a cause for violent behavior. Medical researchers found that children with low self-esteem lack a chemical produced by the brain called seratonin. "Self-esteem is absolutely chemically based," says Dr. Forrest Tenant, a public health specialist in California. Vitamins, minerals, and other nutrients allow the body to make seratonin. "You test a successful athlete, and he has very high degrees of seratonin because he eats properly. You test a gang member or a juvenile offender or a drug addict, and they have almost none."[13] Dr. Tenant says that most problem kids eat tremendous amounts of carbohydrates—pasta, breads, cereals—and not enough protein. This is not conducive to good mental health.

CHILD ABUSE AND
KIDS WHO KILL

The first teachers a child has are his or her parents. If the parents are violent, the child learns that violence is an acceptable behavior when angry, stressed, disappointed, or frustrated. Studies show that children who are abused and neglected are at high risk for committing violence. These children fail to develop a trusting, loving relationship with their parents, because they withdraw from parents in fear of getting beaten, rather than moving closer to them to confide in or share activities with them.

A teenage inmate at the Ventura Lockup in California explained her violent behavior this way: "I didn't have anyone to care about me. I didn't think I was good or important. So since nobody showed me I was important, I didn't care about anybody else. I wanted everybody else to be as low as I was."[14]

A teenage boy at the Ventura Lockup said, "It's hard for a kid coming up without a male role model in the house. I had older brothers who were involved in gangs and the whole dope life. I never even met my father. My mother's my father."[15]

GUNS AND KIDS WHO KILL

Years ago when teenagers fought, they fought with fists. Now they fight with guns. What was then a bruise to the face or a hurt ego is now death or a paralyzing injury. In the United States, more people die of gunshot wounds every two years than died in the entire Vietnam War. There are more gun dealers in America than there are gas stations. Thus, it is not surprising that although America's overall crime rate has declined over the last decade, the death rate from firearms has risen.[16]

According to the Department of Justice, the average cost of a handgun bought from a street source is $100 or less and that of an assault rifle $300 or less. A survey of 835 male serious offenders in four states revealed that 55 percent had carried guns all the time in the year or two before being jailed. The firearms most used were high-powered revolvers. Automatic and semiautomatic handguns closely rivaled those weapons in popularity.[17]

A fourteen-year-old girl said, "It's easy to find a gun. You're thinking this person [is] gonna hurt me. So I'm gonna get me something in my protection. I ended up killing a girl. I didn't mean to. But I was held accountable because I pulled the trigger."[18]

TEENS ON TARGET

Because of the countless crippling injuries he saw among California's youth, Dr. Luis Montes started a group named Teens on Target. "It's devastating to talk to families and tell them that their son or daughter is never going to walk again. We have to look at guns as the lethal link in this chain of violence. So we thought, what could be better than to have victims of violence communicate with other youth about stopping the epidemic of violence."[19]

One of the objectives of Teens on Target is to educate lawmakers about gun violence. Dr. Montes believes legislators are influenced by the National Rifle Association (NRA), a powerful pro-gun lobbyist group whose influence has kept legislators from voting for gun control laws. A slogan that the NRA is known for is "Guns do not kill people.

People kill people." Schanell Sorrells, whose unborn baby was killed by a gun, and other gunshot victims like her, would undoubtedly argue that guns do indeed kill people.

MAKING GUNS SAFER

Johnny, fourteen, liked to load his father's shotgun. One day he decided to play Russian roulette. He randomly loaded the gun with five cartridges, three live shells and two dummies, and asked his friends to play. He then pointed the gun at Gabriel, thirteen, and pumped the shotgun, not knowing whether the shell he chambered was live or a dummy. He then pulled the trigger, firing a live round, which tore through Gabriel's chest and lungs, killing him. Although Johnny claimed the killing was an accident, he was convicted of "depraved indifference murder."[20]

Physicians who treat gunshot wounds are calling for "childproofing" guns to make them impossible to be fired by a young child. One suggestion is to use a method invented in the late 1880s, a "grip safety." The part of the gun that would be in the palm of the hand had a lever that had to be depressed before the trigger could be pulled. The reason the gun was childproof was that a small child's hand is too small and weak to depress the lever and pull the trigger at the same time.

Another suggestion is to personalize guns so that only the authorized user can shoot it. One way to do this would be to have the authorized user wear a ring or bracelet that communicates either electronically or magnetically with the gun so the gun will operate only when held by the person wearing the ring. Many crimes are committed with guns stolen out of homes during burglaries. Thus, if a gun is stolen this way, it will be useless to the burglar or to anyone he or she tries to sell the gun to.

Guns are the second-leading cause of death among Americans age ten to nineteen. Accidental shootings by very young children could be prevented if guns were childproofed, making the guns difficult to discharge by small, weak hands.

HATE CRIMES

On the evening of December 19, 1986, three African-American men were driving through a white neighborhood of New York City called Howard Beach. Their car broke down and they took off on foot looking for help. A mob of white teenagers attacked them. Two of the men escaped after being severely beaten with fists, bats, and tree limbs. The third man was beaten and then chased into the path of an oncoming car, which struck and killed him. Jason Ladone, eighteen, and John Lester and Scott Kern, both seventeen, were convicted of manslaughter. Lester was sentenced to serve from ten to thirty years in prison, Kern received six to eighteen years, and Ladone five to fifteen years.[22]

In another incident, up to forty youths in New York City's Bensonhurst neighborhood attacked Yusef Hawkins, a black sixteen-year-old, and his friends in 1989. Hawkins had gone to Bensonhurst to look at a used car. Within minutes of leaving the subway, he was shot to death by one of the white youths.[23]

In 1991, still another hate-motivated murder committed by a kid occurred in the racially mixed neighborhood of Crown Heights, in Brooklyn, New York. On August 19, an Orthodox rabbi accidentally ran over and killed Gavin Cato, a seven-year-old black boy. The death sparked a four-day riot in which blacks attacked Jews in the neighborhood. During the riots, twenty-nine-year-old Yankel Rosenbaum, an Hassidic Jewish student visiting from Melbourne, Australia, was attacked by black youths, chased, and then stabbed to death by sixteen-year-old Lemrick Nelson, a black teenager.

The case drew national headlines because of claims the murder was not investigated properly and that Rosenbaum did not receive proper medical attention. In 1992, Nelson was acquitted in criminal court, by a mostly black jury, angering Jewish leaders to demand federal intervention. Two years later, Attorney General Janet Reno ordered a civil rights investigation into the crime. That investigation led to a civil trial charging Nelson with violating Rosenbaum's civil rights. In that trial, which began on January 16, 1997, forty-three-year-old Charles Price, a black man, was also indicted for inciting blacks to attack Jews during the 1991 riots, which prosecutors say may have led to Rosenbaum's fatal stabbing. Both men were found guilty on February 10, 1997. They face life in prison.[24]

Hate crimes—acts of violence against people purely because of their race, religion, ethnic background, or sexual orientation—are one of the fastest-growing kinds of violent crime in the United States. And more often than not, teenagers are the perpetrators. Estimates are that between 10,000 and 40,000 hate crimes are committed annually in the United States—primarily by white males in their teens or early twenties.[25] New York City, one of the few cities that keeps track of bias-related crimes, reports that between 1986 and 1990, 70 percent of people arrested for hate crimes were under nineteen.

WHITE SUPREMACIST GROUPS

White supremacist groups—white organizations formed to make America all white and all Christian—attack people of minority races and of religions other than Christianity. Their main goal is to start a racial holy war in which they will kill all nonwhites and non-Christians. One type of white supremacist group, called skinheads because of their shaved heads, is composed mainly of males in their teens and early twenties. Skinheads wear swastika tattoos and have adopted a creed of violence against Jews, blacks, gays, and other minorities. Other white supremacist groups include the Ku Klux Klan, the Aryan Nation, and the White Aryan Resistance, headed by onetime Klansman David Metzger, whose philosophy includes the expulsion of America's Latinos and Asians and the creation of separate black and white states.

In July 1996, youths in a white supremacist group called the Lords of Chaos went to their music teacher's house and knocked on the door. When he answered, they killed him with a shotgun blast in the face. The reason? He had caught them planning to burn the school auditorium.[26] In Birmingham, Alabama, three teen skinheads spotted a homeless black man asleep on the street. They woke him, then knifed him to death in celebration of Hitler's birthday.[27] A new kind of murder by skinheads is what they call a "boot party," in which a group of skinheads stomp to death a person of racial minority. One such boot party occurred in 1990 in Houston, Texas, when two teen skinheads stomped a fifteen-year-old Vietnamese immigrant to death.[28]

Why do teenagers commit hate murders? One explanation is that such killings make kids feel like they belong to an "in group" that opposes people who are different. In the 1930s, Adolph Hitler rose to power by convincing his followers that the economic depression in Germany was the fault of the Jews. He claimed the way to stop the depression was to rid the country of everyone who was not an Aryan (white Christian). Many of today's impoverished youth who have no hope of going to college or getting a decent job also look for a scapegoat (someone to blame) for their poor living conditions. They believe that if they kill the minorities they hold responsible for keeping them from living the good life, then all their problems will go away.

Much of the roots of hate crimes come from messages teens get from adults. There is a saying that "you have to be taught to hate," meaning children are not born prejudiced; rather, they *learn* to hate by imitating the behavior of adults in their environment. If kids hear racial slurs over the dinner table every night, they learn that these words are as acceptable as saying "please" and "thank you." Many kids who commit hate crimes are acting out the beliefs they got from home.

VIOLENCE IN THE MEDIA

By the time he or she finishes elementary school, the average American child witnesses 8,000 murders and 200,000 other acts of violence on TV and in the movies. While many children learn about violence in their real-life families, they also grow up surrounded by simulated violence. Powerful images pour into their lives in the form of violent movies, TV shows, video games, music videos, and local news shows replaying every headline murder over and over throughout the day.

Kids learn by observation and imitation. For example, they watch and copy their teachers writing the alphabet on the chalkboard, a quarterback making a touchdown, or a gymnast mastering the balance beam. What happens when they watch someone being brutally murdered on television or in the movies? The screen becomes their teacher, and what they learn is that not only is violence normal but often the most violent acts are committed by the hero of the show.

Sometimes what kids learn from the media gives them another reason to kill. A prime example is the TV commercial for Nike sneakers, featuring basketball star Michael Jordan going for a 360-degree slam dunk. Afterward his loyal fan Mars Blackmon, played by filmmaker Spike Lee, says, "How'd he do that? It's got to be the shoes."[29]

For some kids, the reason they *kill* is the shoes. This

commercial has made Nike's Air Jordan sneakers the ultimate status symbol among inner-city kids. A growing number of murders are occurring in which kids kill other kids over their sneakers or other status-symbol clothes such as varsity jackets and leather coats. Many teens dress to impress. But many of the hottest fashions are very expensive, especially for inner-city kids. A pair of Air Jordans, for example, can cost $140.[30]

Critics say companies like Nike have a moral obligation to address the problem. The Reverend Tyrone Crider, director of Operation PUSH, a civil rights organization in Chicago, said, "Nike continues to exploit our youth for money while they [Jordan and Lee] go on pitching items that are getting people who look up to them killed."[31] In response, Spike Lee said, "These senseless crimes are occurring not because of an advertising campaign, but because the people who are doing the killing have screwed-up values. To them, life is cheap because they don't feel life has anything to offer."[32] Lee is now featured in a new series of commercials advising young people to stay in school and make something of themselves.

MOVIES AND TV

The most popular plot in movies and TV dramas today is murder, in its most bloody, savage form. The movie *Natural Born Killers,* about a young boy and girl who kill for the fun of it, has been blamed for several similar murders in the United States. On television, the cartoon characters Beavis and Butthead burned their house down, teaching kids that violent, illegal acts are funny and okay.

Or, at almost any movie theater today, not only is the major feature about serial killers who perform savage acts on their victims but before the feature even starts, trailers for upcoming films are filled with plots about murder, with the starring role going to the murderer. How do kids behave in their real lives when they learn from the media that if you want power, money, and respect, use violence?

George Modica, a member of Teens on Target, explained his violent acts this way: "I can remember being eight or nine years old looking at Al Capone. . . . And I would see how he would do drive-bys, and that would influence my behavior as well as my friends'. They had machine guns . . . it intrigued me . . . I developed a fantasy for guns, so I joined a gang. A lot of kids see these movies and want to get a gun and use it."[33]

The reason violence grabs our attention is that we have an emotional response to it. Violence stimulates an adrenaline rush. And things that stimulate an adrenaline rush get us to pay attention. In video games such as "Mortal Kombat," a player wins by blasting the most people to pieces. As players get better at the game, they can deal lethal blows to their opponents by ripping out imaginary vital organs and "snapping" the opponent's spine.

GANGSTER RAP

Rap music started as a kind of verbal, good-natured wordplay about life in the inner cities. Then in the mid-1980s, young black males in the inner cities of Los Angeles, fed up with the poverty, unemployment, drug abuse, and gang violence rampant in the ghettoes, invented a new kind of music. Called *rap*, the lyrics advocated murder and violence as a way to express their anger. In the early 1990s, an even more hard-core rap, called *gangster rap* or *gangsta rap*, developed in the poverty-ridden areas of southern California, such as Compton, Long Beach, and South-Central Los Angeles. Many of these 90s rappers are drug dealers, pimps, or gang members, who are often charged with the same crimes their lyrics promote.

Violence in rapper songs has generated violence in real life. For example, rapper Snoop Doggy Dogg was charged, but later acquitted, in 1996 of a gang-related murder. In 1994, rapper Tupac Shakur, whose lyrics allegedly inspired a Texas murder, was shot outside a New York City recording studio being used by Sean "Puffy" Combs, head of the East Coast recording company, Bad Boy Entertainment. Shakur survived and accused Combs of being behind the attack.

Later that year, Tupac Shakur was convicted of sexual abuse. In 1995, while still in prison, he signed with Suge Knight and his West Coast L.A.-based Death Row Records. (Knight himself is now serving nine years in prison for violating probation on an assault conviction.) Tupac immediately released a song that threatened the Bad Boy label rappers with violent retaliation for his being shot. Thus, tensions mounted between rappers of the two labels. Released from prison in 1996, Shakur was killed in a drive-by shooting on September 7, 1996, in Las Vegas, Nevada.[34]

Although there are officially no suspects in Shakur's murder, officials with East Coast Death Row Records believe a member of the Crips street gang was responsible, as the Crips have close ties to officials and rappers of West Coast Bad Boy records, and hired Crips members as bodyguards during visits to the West Coast. This belief is further justified in the minds of Death Row officials because the Crips are bitter rivals of the Bloods gang, who have close ties with rappers and officials of Death Row Records.

Six months after Shakur's murder, another gangster rapper was murdered, Christopher "Biggie Smalls" Wallace, or "B.I.G.," as he was also named for his 6 ft.-3 in., 300-pound size. On March 9, 1997, Biggie was attending a party at the Peterson Automotive Museum in Los Angeles to celebrate the Soul Train Music Awards. Around midnight the fire marshal ordered the party shut down because of overcrowding in the building. Seconds after Biggie and a friend left the parking lot in Biggie's truck, a gunman in a passing car shot him with a 9-mm handgun. Biggie died on the way to the hospital.

Like Shakur, Biggie glorified death in his lyrics. In his song, "You're Nobody," he raps, "You're nobody till somebody kills you."[35] Officials of Bad Boy Records believe Biggie was killed by a Bloods gang member in retaliation for Shakur's murder. However, the L.A.P.D. insists it is focusing its investigation on the same Crips members who were bodyguards for the Bad Boy rappers.

Kids in both the ghettos and more affluent neighborhoods idolize rappers as heroes and take violent gangster rap to heart. Many kids cannot separate the murderous lyrics promoted on CDs from how they should act in real life. Says C. DeLores Tucker, chairperson of the National Political Congress of Black Women, "Our kids have adopted the gangsta culture as a direct result of this music. We have kids killing kids, little boys raping little girls. . . ."[36]

Some rappers are calling for a reevaluation of violence in their songs. Says rapper Wyclef of the band the Fugees: "We all need to chill out for a second and step back. . . ."[37] Other rappers are calling for an end to gangsta rap altogether. In a hip-hop summit in Harlem, speakers talked about how gangsta rap becomes like a drug in a young person's life. Said one speaker, "Rap is a vehicle for youth to express themselves. But the negativity is destroying what these young rappers have built."[38] Tavis Smiley, author of *Hard Left,* a collection of political essays, agrees, saying, "The value of life is decreasing by the minute right in front of kids' eyes."[39]

FIGHTING VIOLENCE IN THE MEDIA

Many communities are taking action to fight violence in the media. For example, in Minneapolis, Minnesota, each week there is a "turn off the violence day," in which citizens try to get people not to watch violence, whether a music video, a newscast, or a TV show. Their theory is that turning off violence for one day shows you can control violence by preventing it from coming into your home. Such control inspires people to think about other things they can do to stop violence.

Many people are trying to combat violence by organizing community groups to campaign for quality TV programming. They urge advertisers not to sponsor TV programs that emphasize violence, and recommend parents keep their kids from watching violent programs by using electronic blocking/locking devices on their televisions. UCLA professor James Q. Wilson says, "I think the most troubling problem this nation may face is . . . the fact we are increasingly raising our children in isolation from human contact. We are turning over to electronic devices, from TV programs to electronic games, the task of occupying ourselves. To the extent that we eliminate human interactions, we are reducing the chances that we will learn what it means to be fully human. . . ."[40]

Declared former surgeon general Dr. C. Everett Koop in a recent editorial in the *Journal of the American Medical Association*, "We believe violence in America to be a public health emergency. . . ."[41] Dr. Koop is right. Today's kids are killing for every reason imaginable—from survival, to envy of someone else's Nike sneakers, to the elimination of rival drug sellers, to mere kicks—often as an outgrowth of violence and abuse dealt them from their own families.

THREE

MURDER IN
THE FAMILY

IN THE EARLY EVENING of August 20, 1989, brothers Lyle and
Erik Menendez, ages twenty-one and eighteen, stood outside their home—their parents' Beverly Hills, California,
mansion—and loaded their shotguns. Their parents, Jose
and Kitty, were in the family's den watching television.
Guns ready, the brothers burst into the den and started firing. Jose was killed instantly, but Kitty, shot in the head,
was still alive. Lyle put his shotgun next to her head and
fired one more time, finishing her off.

Then, to provide them an alibi, the brothers went to a
movie in Santa Monica. Afterward, they returned home and
phoned the police, shouting they had found their parents
murdered. They claimed the slayings were a mob hit aimed
at their father, a film executive. The Menendez brothers almost got away with the "perfect crime." But Erik, feeling
guilty and depressed over the murders, confessed the story
on tape to his therapist, psychologist Jerome Oziel. Patient-
therapist privilege prevented Dr. Oziel from telling anyone.
His mistress, Judalon Smyth, however, had no such restric-

tions. When her relationship with Oziel ended in March 1990, she told police she had overheard Erik confess to Oziel. Police arrested Lyle and Erik.

Although the brothers could be considered adults (eighteen and over), their crime was considered by many people to be the result of years of childhood problems. Therefore, the murders were also considered a case of juvenile homicide by the public.

During the trial, which began in 1993, the brothers were tried together, but with two separate juries, because some of the evidence applied to one brother and not the other. The prosecution claimed the motive was greed, as the brothers stood to inherit $14 million. The defense claimed the shootings were in self-defense to escape years of child abuse and sexual molestation by their parents. In January 1994, both juries deadlocked and a mistrial was declared.[1]

THE ABUSE EXCUSE

The deadlock sparked a national debate over what came to be called the "Abuse Excuse." Shortly after Erik and Lyle were arrested, Erik's attorney, Leslie Abramson, asked forensic psychiatrist Dr. William Vicary to evaluate Lyle and Erik. In his meetings with Dr. Vicary, Erik claimed his father had physically and sexually abused him since age five, sticking tacks in his buttocks and thighs, forcing him to have oral sex, and sodomizing him. Erik said his father threatened to beat him to death if he told anyone.

Lyle said that a few days before the killings, he confronted Jose about his abuse of Erik and Jose warned him not to challenge his authority. Lyle took this as a threat that Jose would kill him if he told, so he persuaded Erik they needed to buy shotguns for protection. Lyle claimed that his father's insistence that the boys go on a family yachting trip meant that Jose had decided to kill them anyway while on the yacht and make it look like an accident. Lyle allegedly told Erik they had to kill both parents before Jose killed them.

After listening to the brothers, Dr. Vicary concluded they were emotionally immature but not mentally ill. However, he knew kids rarely kill their parents, and when they do, it is usually because of extreme abuse over a long period of time. Thus was born the Abuse Excuse.[2]

THE RETRIAL

A new set of prosecutors was appointed for the retrial of the Menendez brothers, which began October 13, 1995, before a single jury. This time, the prosecution focused on proving the brothers' claim they killed their parents after years of abuse was a defense concocted after their carefully crafted murder alibi became unraveled.

A new piece of evidence in the retrial was a letter Lyle wrote to Amir Eslaminia, whose father, Hedeyat, was murdered in 1984 by members of the infamous Billionaire Boys Club. The letter outlined the lies Lyle wanted Amir to testify to during the first trial. A new witness was Klara Wright, whose son played on the tennis circuit with Erik. She testified that upon her arrival at the Menendez mansion the morning after the killings, Erik asked her if her husband, an attorney, handled wills and probate cases. Mrs. Wright described Erik as being so excited he could not get the words out fast enough. Erik spent that night at her home, bringing with him the safe the brothers believed contained their parents' wills.

Pathologist Robert Laurence used wooden mannequins pierced with metal rods to illustrate the angles of the shotgun blasts in relation to the bodies of Jose and Kitty. The

Lyle (*left*) and Erik Menendez in a courtroom in Beverly Hills, California, prior to their preliminary hearing on charges of murdering their parents

mannequins demonstrated the victims were shot first in the head, not the legs. This testimony supported the prosecution's contention that the brothers shot to kill (the head wounds), and only afterward inflicted wounds to their parents' legs to mimic a mob hit.[3]

REBUTTING THE ABUSE EXCUSE

In the first trial, the prosecution did not call one mental health expert to rebut the defense's abuse excuse. In the retrial, however, the prosecution called in a powerful mental health witness, Dr. Park Elliott Dietz, a forensic psychiatrist who had testified for the FBI and CIA in several high-profile trials, including that of serial killer Jeffrey Dahmer and John Hinckley, the would-be assassin of former President Reagan.

Dietz disputed the abuse excuse by testifying he did not

agree with the defense psychiatrist's diagnosis that Erik and Lyle killed their parents out of fear resulting from a lifetime of sexual, physical, and psychological abuse. "Instead, I'm diagnosing generalized anxiety disorder," Dietz said; that far less severe illness is characterized by "excessive anxiety and worry that occurs more days than not over six months."[4] In addition, Dietz testified that Erik showed signs of personality disorders, including being overly self-dramatizing, histrionic, fearful of abandonment, unconcerned with the truth, and disrespectful of the law.

Dietz's testimony sharply contradicted defense expert John Wilson, a Cleveland State University professor and leading expert in "post-traumatic stress disorder" (PTSD). Wilson claimed Erik could not leave his abusive environment because he suffered from "learned helplessness," a symptom of PTSD. Dietz countered by saying the fact that Erik bought a shotgun, loaded the weapon, and went to a shooting range to learn to fire the weapon showed assertive behavior not found in the passiveness of a person with learned helplessness.

Dietz said he could neither accept nor dispute Erik's medically unprovable story that Jose Menendez sexually brutalized him from ages six to eighteen. And without a known traumatic event, such as sexual molestation, there can be no diagnosis of PTSD. He also disputed the defense's panic theory, saying people undergoing panic attacks usually run *away* from the source of their anxiety, not *toward* it as the Menendez brothers did when they burst in on their parents and killed them.[5]

THE FLANNEL DEFENSE

The defense sought manslaughter convictions under a legal concept known as "imperfect self-defense," also known as the "Flannel Defense." The term comes from the case of *The People v. Flannel,* in which Justice Rose Bird of the California Supreme Court ruled that a person who kills another in the honest, but unreasonable, belief in the necessity to defend against imminent peril to life is not guilty of murder but rather of manslaughter.

This means even if the jurors believed there was no threat to the brothers' lives, if *Lyle and Erik* believed there was a threat—no matter how crazy that belief was—they could not be found guilty of murder but only of manslaughter.[6] The sole issue of the Flannel Defense was whether the boys' fear was honest. The prosecution claimed the brothers decided to falsely use the Flannel Defense while in jail, when their original denial of involvement was shown to be a lie and they were arrested.[7]

Erik's attorney, Leslie Abramson, in her closing argument, told the jury the boys murdered their parents "out of mind-numbing, adrenaline-pumping fear their parents would kill them first for threatening to expose the dysfunctional family's secrets."[8] On March 20, 1996, the jury reached a verdict: guilty of first-degree murder. And on April 17, 1996, the jury decided to spare the brothers' lives by voting for the penalty of life in prison without the possibility of parole instead of the death penalty.[9]

What makes kids like Erik and Lyle Menendez commit murders? So many families today use violence to settle arguments and express anger that kids learn violent behavior along with the ABCs. Instead of seeing their parents and other family members talk about angry feelings, they see family members hit, punch, throw things, and even use weapons against anyone who angers them. Every year, 3 million children ages three to seventeen are exposed to parental violence.[10] Studies show children who witness violence to be at greater risk to commit violence themselves.

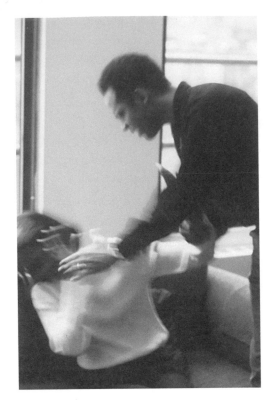

Children who grow up in families where one parent expresses anger through violent behavior toward the other parent are at greater risk to commit violence themselves.

Growing up with a steady diet of abuse, rejection, and neglect can inflict lasting psychological wounds. Such children often become withdrawn, mistrustful, defensive, and violent. They can suffer depression and anxiety for years.[11]

KIDS WHO KILL THEIR PARENTS

There are several reasons why kids kill their parents. Many murder for revenge against or escape from a parent who is psychologically, physically, or sexually abusive. In fact, more children are in jail today for killing an abusive parent than for drive-by shootings or drug deals. Other kids kill family members as a result of violent reactions to drug or alcohol abuse, or violence due to the early stages of mental illness.

Still other kids murder parents during violent arguments.

Statistics show that more than half of juveniles who murder family members are motivated by an argument, and 64 percent of them use a firearm.[12] Sons kill their parents more often than daughters, and the parent most kids of either gender kill is the father.[13]

These kids who kill feel unappreciated and misunderstood, are jealous, and are easily angered by minor slights. "Around them, we feel edgy, as though we're walking on eggshells, waiting for them to blow up," says Douglas H. Powell, a psychologist at Harvard University.[14] For most kids, episodes of anger are relatively mild and brief. However, for a small group of kids, extreme violent reactions to parents' rules are the norm. They see their parents' demands as unreasonable.

These kids usually have no history of delinquency and do not share the classic characteristics of the violently aggressive juvenile delinquent. For example, one day a fourteen-year-old Glendale, California, boy who had never been in trouble before and was regarded as a quiet, polite kid, told some friends he felt like shooting someone. He went home and shot his mother to death. Then he went to a phone booth and called 911 to confess.[15]

During almost all his seventeen years, Dale Whipple of Indiana was physically, psychologically, and sexually abused by his parents. Even though he sought help from school guidance counselors, no one did anything to stop the abuse. Finally, Dale decided he could take no more. He lured his mother into the garage and hacked her to death with an ax. Then he went into the house and axed his sleeping father. Charged with two counts of murder, Dale claimed self-defense, saying he killed his parents to protect himself from his father's increasingly severe beatings and his mother's sexual advances. Although the judge concluded that fear of future physical abuse was a factor in the murders, he refused to allow the jury to consider Dale's plea of self-defense. Dale was sentenced to two concurrent sentences of forty years in prison. He will be eligible for parole after serving twenty years.[16]

KIDS AS HIT MEN

In some cases of family killings by juveniles, a kid asks a nonfamily member to kill a member of his or her family. One such case was made into a TV movie. On February 6, 1986, at 6:00 A.M., James Pierson, a forty-two-year-old widower from Long Island, New York, was gunned down in front of his home by seventeen-year-old Sean Pica. Sean was a classmate of Mr. Pierson's sixteen-year-old daughter, Cheryl, a popular high school cheerleader. Three months earlier, Sean and Cheryl had discussed a newspaper article about a battered woman who hired someone to kill her abusive husband. Sean said he would kill someone for the right price. Cheryl offered him $1,000 to kill her father. Sean accepted and received a $400 down payment from Cheryl's boyfriend.[17]

After an intense investigation, police suspected Sean of the murder and confronted him. He confessed and pleaded guilty to manslaughter and was sentenced to eight to twenty-four years in prison. Cheryl's boyfriend was sentenced to five years' probation for his part in the murder. Cheryl Pierson also pleaded guilty but received no sentence, allowing her to be released from jail after only 106 days. Why? When Cheryl was twelve, her father began sexually abusing her. At the time of the murder, Cheryl feared her father was about to begin sexually abusing her younger sister as well. In sentencing her, the judge took into consideration Cheryl's years of abuse.[18]

In other cases, kids kill an abusive parent to protect or please the nonabusive parent. Sometimes these kids are subtly encouraged to murder by the nonabusive parent. In February 1987, eleven-year-old Mary Baily shot and killed her stepfather. Both Mary and her mother, Priscilla Wyers, were charged in the murder. Mary told the jury her stepfather physically abused Priscilla and that Priscilla asked her to kill him. The morning of the murder, Priscilla took Mary into the living room where her stepfather was asleep. A loaded rifle was lying nearby. Mary took the rifle and shot him. She was placed in a state foster home. Her mother was convicted of first-degree murder.[19]

In still other instances, kids kill parents during a confrontation with them while high on drugs or alcohol. A New York boy stabbed his mother to death when she refused to give him $200 to feed his crack habit. In another case, Wesley Underwood, fifteen, shot and killed his mother during an argument about whether he had misplaced her knitting needle. Wesley, a loner addicted to heavy-metal music, had been drinking and sniffing gasoline fumes shortly before the argument began. He pleaded guilty and was sentenced to eighteen years in prison.[20]

KIDS WHO KILL SIBLINGS

Other family homicides committed by kids involve murders of siblings. And when siblings murder siblings, the victim is usually a brother. Most of these killings are impulsive acts of revenge or jealousy. In many cases, the perpetrator is a dis-

turbed, abused child who has previously tried unsuccessfully to kill a sibling. The easy availability of guns in the
home is a major factor in homicides committed by kids.
These murders usually occur when one child becomes involved in an argument with a sibling and reaches for a gun
to settle the dispute. For example, Dr. Kay Tooley reported
on two neglected and abused six-year-olds who tried repeatedly to kill their siblings. Mary, who was sexually abused by
her mother's boyfriend, set fire to her younger brother and
then tried to pour liquid bleach down her infant half-sister's
throat. Jay, who was often beaten by his father, set fire to his
sister's dress and held her head underwater in a swimming
pool. Both Mary's and Jay's parents were unconcerned with
their children's murderous behavior.[21]

In April 1985, nine-year-old Britt Kellum got into an
argument with his eleven-year-old brother. Britt took his
father's shotgun and killed his brother. Finding Britt too
young to be held accountable, juvenile authorities ordered
him to undergo counseling. Four years later, Britt shot his
six-year-old brother to death with his father's .38-caliber
handgun, which his father had taught him to shoot and had
left where he could get it. According to the law, because
Britt was tried as a child for the murder, he will be released
from juvenile prison on his twenty-first birthday.[22]

In another case, sixteen-year-old Timothy Duane Brown
had been expelled from high school for threatening a student with a switchblade. His parents punished him by not
allowing him to see or phone his girlfriend. When his
eleven-year-old kid brother caught him using the phone behind his parents' backs, the teenager beat the boy to death
with a baseball bat, then shot and killed his grandmother
and stepfather with a deer rifle. The teenager was tried as
an adult and sentenced to life in prison.[23]

Other times, the killings are accidental. They usually

occur when a child is playing with a gun and accidentally fires it, killing a sibling, friend, or someone else who happens to be in the line of fire.

MENTALLY ILL KIDS
WHO KILL FAMILY MEMBERS

On September 16, 1985, John Justice, a seventeen-year-old high school honor student in Buffalo, New York, stabbed his mother, brother, and father to death, then rammed his father's car into the back of another car, killing the driver, a neighbor. Over the next two hours, John tried unsuccessfully to slit his wrists with a razor blade. Psychiatrists testified John hated his mother, was upset over his parents' refusal to pay for his college expenses, and suffered from a personality disorder. For murdering his father and brother, the jury found him not guilty by reason of insanity, but guilty for killing his mother and neighbor.[24]

In a much publicized case, on September 8, 1984, fifteen-year-old Patrick DeGelleke of Rochester, New York, set his adoptive parents' home on fire as they slept, burning them to death. Years before the killing, Patrick had been diagnosed with behavioral and emotional problems and had been in counseling. At school he could not concentrate and stared off into space for hours. At home he was withdrawn but would sometimes erupt into violent, uncontrollable temper tantrums.

His parents took him to court, claiming he was involved in truancy and theft and that they could not control him. According to a psychologist who testified at his trial, his parents' actions made Patrick fear he would be institutionalized, which sent him into a psychotic rage during which he lost his sense of reality and set the fire. The jury rejected Patrick's insanity plea and found him guilty of murder.[25]

Sergeant Mark Wynn, head of a domestic violence program in Nashville, Tennessee, believes in order to stop kids from killing family members, domestic violence has to be stopped. He knows what he is talking about, as he grew up in a violent home. He tried to kill his stepfather when he was seven years old to stop him from beating his mother.

"Children learn to be violent, and they bring it into their adult life," he says. "We were taught to be violent by my stepfather. Many times, the police came to my home, and many times they walked away. Many times, the neighbors heard the screams and saw the fights in the yard, but never called the police. Not just the police, but the community, prosecutors, social services, churches, schools . . . everybody has to wake up. And say until we hold people accountable in the family, we're going to keep generating kids who kill year after year after year."[26]

FOUR

MURDER IN THE NEIGHBORHOOD

AFTER A RAINSTORM, four-year-old Derrick Robie used to dig for worms in the yard of his Savona, New York, home. In the winter, he used to stuff hickory nuts into his coat pockets. He used to play teeball and soccer, help his dad mix meat loaf, and his mom wash the family car. Derrick does not do any of these things anymore. For early on August 2, 1993, he met thirteen-year-old Eric Smith.

Three days a week, Derrick went to a summer recreation program in a field at the end of his dead-end street. That morning, dark clouds threatened rain. Derrick's baby brother, Dalton, was fussing, and his mother was taking longer than usual to walk Derrick to day camp. He begged her to let him go by himself. There were always lots of kids walking along the street, so his mother said okay. Derrick blew her a kiss and was gone.

As Derrick walked down the block, Eric Smith rode by on his bike. A chunky kid with glasses, red hair, and a spray of freckles, Eric played drums in the school band. He told

Derrick he would take him on a shortcut to day camp, then led him into an empty lot, overgrown with pine trees. About 9:20 A.M. Mary Davidson, who lives two houses away from the park, heard a child scream. When she ran outside, she saw two cats and assumed the cry came from them. She noticed Eric riding by on his bike about 9:30 A.M., as she was leaving for work.

About 11:00 A.M., the rain that had been threatening all morning finally unleashed itself on the town. Day camp was called off, and Derrick's mother went to pick him up. When the director told her Derrick had never arrived, she frantically checked neighbors' houses. Not finding him, she notified the police. Within hours, a search was under way. Police brought in helicopters, and residents came home from work early to join the search. Ted Smith, Eric's stepfather, was one of the volunteers.

Derrick's body was found that afternoon in the field behind Mary Davidson's property. That night, Eric stayed at the home of a family friend, Marlene Haskell. She said he seemed afraid. He asked her what would happen if the killer turned out to be a kid. Marlene told Eric's mother, Tammy, but she did not take his comment seriously. However, when police still had no suspect after three days, the two women took Eric to the police, thinking he might have seen someone with Derrick before the murder and could identify the person to authorities.

Eric at first denied even seeing Derrick that day but later admitted he had seen the child. He said he had not been wearing his glasses, yet he was able to describe in detail Derrick's clothing and lunch bag. "I know he can't see ten feet in front of him," said Marlene Haskell, sure he was lying.[1] Eric's great-grandfather, a retired sheriff's investigator, was also suspicious. Six days after the murder, he had a serious talk with Eric, who finally broke down and confessed. "I asked him why he did it," his mother said. "He just kept saying, 'I don't know, I don't know.'" [2]

That night, his mother took Eric to the police. In a voice without any emotion, he told how he had seen Derrick that morning and knew he wanted to take him someplace and hurt him. Then Eric described the attack in brutal detail: "I put my right arm around his neck. . . . I squeezed harder as the kid made fists and swung his arms trying to get away. . . . He didn't make any more noise, so I let him down on the ground." [3] When Eric stuffed a napkin and plastic bag from Derrick's lunch into his mouth, Derrick bit him. Eric struck him on the head and chest with some rocks, poured Kool-Aid from his own lunch into the wounds, and dragged his body to a rock pile. Then Eric Smith rode off on his bike.

Eric was tried for second-degree murder (unpremeditated) under a New York law that permits thirteen-year-olds accused of homicide to be tried as adults. He was sentenced to nine years to life—the maximum possible penalty for a minor. He will serve at least the first part of his sentence at a lockup for juveniles; he could be transferred to an adult prison at age eighteen and free by age twenty-two.

Why would a thirteen-year-old murder a four-year-old boy? Eric Smith was found to be developmentally slow. As a toddler, he showed delays in walking and talking, and his parents enrolled him in an early education intervention program. He had violent temper tantrums until he was four, holding his breath and banging his head on the floor. Eric admitted he was angry on the morning he killed Derrick Robie. When he saw Derrick on his way to day camp, Eric, unable to hold his anger, felt impelled to act, and killed him.

With his large ears that curl inward, Eric stood out from other children and was the object of cruel teasing. His

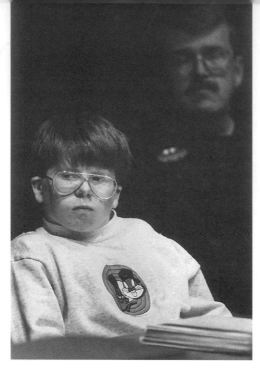

Fourteen-year-old
Eric Smith (*left*)
listens as his lawyer
cross-examines a
forensic psychiatrist
at Eric's trial for the
murder of four-year-old
Derrick Robie, in
the Steuben County
Courthouse in New York
State, in August 1994.

learning problems held him back two years in school. According to his mother, he would complain, "I'm stupid. I'm never going to be anybody."[4] Neighbors say Eric craved attention and that he was afraid of his stepfather. In court, Ted Smith admitted he and his wife argued frequently and that he physically and verbally abused his children, including sexually molesting Eric's fifteen-year-old sister, Stacy.

Psychiatrists who examined Eric concluded he suffers from low self-esteem due in part to his slow development and odd physical features, particularly his protruding ears. Doctors said both abnormalities were caused by an anti-convulsant drug his mother took for epilepsy while pregnant with Eric. Dr. Stephen Herman, a child psychiatrist hired by Eric's defense attorneys, said Eric suffers from depression and "intermittent explosive disorder," a mental disorder that causes uncontrollable explosive outbursts. He cited other factors contributing to Eric's mental illness: a family history of alcoholism and depression, his loneliness, and the physical punishments he endured.

The people in Savona, New York, cleared the base of the hill where Derrick died. His uncle sculpted a bronze statue of Derrick swinging a bat. It stands on a knoll overlooking the town's two new baseball fields. "I hope people can look at the statue and remember what childhood was supposed to be about," said his mother, Doreen. "Because we've lost it somewhere."[5]

Derrick is buried surrounded by the hills of western New York State. His portrait, showing his charming grin, is carved into the headstone. "When Derrick came into this world, I cried," said Derrick's father, Dale. "And when Derrick left this world, I cried."[6] One day shortly after Derrick's death, Doreen opened a little gold box she keeps on the coffee table. Inside she found a hickory nut, placed there by a boy who loved to stuff his pockets with nuts in the winter.

•   •   •

This murder is an example of the senseless killings in American neighborhoods today. Most criminologists blame the easy access to guns as the literal "trigger" to these murders. In many neighborhoods, packing guns is as acceptable as owning a bicycle.

For example, in Queens, New York, Quentin Carter, twelve, asked Brian Wright, sixteen, for a quarter. When Brian refused, the boys got into an argument. The next day, a second argument occurred, and Brian pointed a gun at Quentin and told him to leave him alone. The following day, Quentin and some friends confronted the older boy, who pulled out his gun and shot Quentin. When the boy fell down, Brian shot him three more times.[7]

MURDER IN THE INNER CITY

Although criminal violence affects every segment of society, it falls most heavily on minorities living in poverty-ridden inner cities, where children see murder all the time. They learn the most important lesson in life is to find a way to survive. Unfortunately, the way they find most often is killing. In one recent study of inner-city students ages ten to nineteen, one in four had seen someone killed. African-Americans and Latinos, who most heavily populate the inner cities, are victims of nearly 50 percent of the murders committed every year. In addition, young African-Americans are jailed at a rate three to four times that of young whites, and the rate for young Hispanic men is 60 percent greater than for whites.[8]

Criminologists say poverty is the single most important predictor of criminal violence. Almost 40 percent of black children are raised in poverty, compared to 5 percent of white children. The highest rate of violence occurs in neighborhoods marked by a concentration of poverty and single mothers.[9] These mothers often cannot find jobs and have little or no resources to provide financial security for their children. Add to that the gangs, drug trade, and easy access to guns, and the inner city becomes a war zone where crime is the only employment.

A 1995 survey of 1,591 teenagers in ten inner-city public high schools in California, Louisiana, New Jersey, and Illinois reported the following: 5 percent had used a weapon to commit a crime, 13 percent had dealt drugs, and 22 percent belonged to a gang. In addition, one in five had been attacked with a gun, knife, or other weapon, and two-thirds personally knew someone who had been shot at, stabbed, or assaulted while in school. The students who reported being assaulted or victimized the most were those who belonged to gangs, carried guns, had relatives who carried guns, or who had committed illegal acts such as stealing or selling drugs.[10]

MURDER IN AFFLUENT NEIGHBORHOODS

Inner-city kids are not the only juveniles committing murder in their neighborhood. Kids who live in more affluent areas commit murder as well. Some of these homicides are the result of kids acting out childish emotions, such as jealousy and rage, that turn into murder when children have easy access to guns. For example, a nine-year-old boy shot and killed a seven-year-old girl as she whizzed by on a snowmobile because he wanted to get even with her for bragging about being better than him at Nintendo. Or, jealous of expensive items other kids own, some kids kill over designer jewelry, tennis shoes, jackets, rock concert tickets, and seats in movie theaters. In Detroit, Michigan, for example, a fifteen-year-old boy was shot for his $86 basketball shoes.[11]

How can kids kill anyone over anything, much less over clothes and other material things? One reason is that these kids feel no remorse for taking another person's life. Psychologically, this insensitivity to other people's feelings plays a major role in kids' committing more than one murder. If kids can learn to empathize, or feel what another feels, the chance of their repeating their murders is reduced dramatically.

Many juvenile facilities now teach aggression-control techniques in behavioral modification classes. In role-playing sessions, kids take the parts of both their victims and themselves to reenact their crimes. In almost all cases, these kids end the session feeling for the first time the pain and fear of their victims.

PROFILE OF A
REMORSELESS YOUNG KILLER

Lamar Proby was fourteen in 1991 when he killed the sales clerk of a fashion boutique while robbing the store. Proby grew up in the ghettos of South-Central Los Angeles and first got into trouble after his parents separated when he was eleven. Lamar moved in with his father, thinking he was less strict than his mother. He was right. With his father at work all day and no one to supervise him after school, he could do whatever he wanted. Lamar joined a gang. He loved the excitement of robbing stores and used the money he stole to buy Nike shoes and clothes. If he needed to be somewhere across town, he simply stole a car. Instead of going to school, he went to "ditching parties," composed of groups of kids skipping school that day. If school officials called about his truancy, he erased the message before his father got home.

Lamar bought a .25-caliber gun for $50 from a friend who kept a stash of weapons in his car trunk. "I knew right from wrong," he said. "But my plan was not getting caught."[12] One October afternoon in 1991, he and his friends robbed a fashion boutique. While one friend grabbed jewelry out of a case, Lamar pointed his gun at the sales clerk. "I pushed him against the wall, and then I tried to open the cash register. He came toward me and tried to grab the gun. I shot him in the chest. If he got the gun from me, I felt he was going to shoot me with it."[13]

The boys ran to a friend's house to split up the jewelry. Then Lamar went home and slept. Later when he tried to tell his father what happened, his dad did not believe him. The next morning, he moved back in with his mother. The next month, he and his friends robbed a 7-Eleven store. Police chased them to a motel and arrested them. The gun was matched to the one used to kill the fashion boutique clerk. Lamar Proby pleaded guilty to first-degree murder and was sentenced to the California Youth Authority (CYU) for ten years. He is scheduled to be released in 2002, since juvenile offenders in California tried as juveniles can be held only until their twenty-fifth birthday.

Lamar Proby had not hesitated to rob again, as he felt no guilt or remorse for the crimes he had previously committed, including the murder of the store clerk. "I just felt because I didn't know him, why should I feel anything for him," he said.[14] Then one day a counselor at the CYU asked what he would have felt if his father had been the victim. Lamar said he pictured how the man's widow and two kids were feeling and the pain they were going through. Finally he felt sorry for what he had done. "I'd tell them . . . look where I'm at. An institution, jail. You might be having fun out there right now, but when you get locked up here, it ain't no more fun."[15]

MURDER IN THE SCHOOLS

On February 2, 1996, at 2:00 P.M., a fourteen-year-old honor student walked into his math class at Franklin Junior High School in Moses Lake, Washington, opened his trench coat, took out a high-powered rifle, and began firing. When the smoke cleared, the teenager had killed his teacher, Leona Caires, forty-nine, and two students, Arnold Fritz and Manuel Vela, both fourteen. Pandemonium reigned in the school as students ran screaming into the street. People who knew the boy said he cut class frequently, did not like other kids, and had been telling people for days he was extremely angry.[16]

Nationwide, 95 percent of teachers report they have been attacked by students. Nearly a third say they have considered leaving the profession because they are so afraid of violent attacks by students.[17] In response to such fears, teachers are becoming more militant about their safety, demanding protection from habitually disruptive or threatening students. Several states have made assaulting a teacher an automatic felony.

The greatest fear of schoolteachers today is random violence. "The thing that always scared me was not the bullet with my name on it," said Tom Marshall, a high school auto mechanics teacher in Los Angeles. "It was one of those to-whom-it-may concerns."[18] To some teachers, taking a job at an urban school is combat duty. They map out escape routes: a closet to hide in, a back exit to slip through. They keep classroom doors locked and teach students to duck at the sound of gunfire.

I HATE MONDAYS

For Christmas 1978, Brenda Spencer's father gave her a semiautomatic rifle. A month later, the sixteen-year-old high school senior randomly fired the rifle into a crowded elementary school yard across the street from her San Diego, California, home. The principal and janitor were killed as they tried to shield children from the gunfire. Eight children and a police officer were wounded before Brenda stopped shooting. After a six-hour standoff, Brenda surrendered to police.

When asked why she fired into the playground, Brenda said, "I don't like Mondays. Mondays always get me down."[19] She was charged with first-degree murder. Psychiatrists who examined her described Brenda as "a quiet tomboy obsessed with guns, violence, and fantasies of killing police." She pleaded guilty and was sentenced to two concurrent terms of twenty-five years to life in prison.[20]

SHOOTINGS AT DORSEY HIGH

Shortly before 8:00 A.M. on Monday, February 5, 1996, in Los Angeles, a teenage gang member shot and seriously wounded Eddie Gamez, fourteen, and Aldo Dominquez, sixteen, two Dorsey High School students, as they walked to school. The gunman then jumped into a waiting car and sped off. Police speculated that because the victims were Latino and the suspect black, it was possible the attack was in retaliation for a recent shooting of black gang members. The victims were not members of any gang themselves. "They were just walking to school," said Detective Paul Mize. "They were innocent victims."[21]

THE DORSEY SAFE SCHOOL PROJECT

The shootings were especially tragic to School Superintendent Sid Thompson. In 1993, he formed the Dorsey Safe School Project, a liaison between the school, the Los Angeles Police Department's Southwest Division, and various community groups.

The first step toward ensuring a safe school was installing metal detectors on the campus. Next, meetings were held with students to let them talk about gangs and drug danger spots along their routes to school. Afterward, police officers were assigned to these danger spots. The students also pointed out crack houses, and narcotics officers zeroed in on those areas and cleared out the drug traffic. In addition, police patrols in nearby neighborhoods were increased before and after school.

In spite of the shootings, parents of Dorsey students and some school officials maintained their faith in the Dorsey Safe School Project. They pointed out that as a result, crimes against students at Dorsey dropped from nineteen in 1993 to only one in 1994. By 1995, the Los Angeles school district required all fifty high schools to adopt at least part of the Dorsey strategy.[22]

STATISTICS ON THE ROAD TO MURDER

Every day, 135,000 kids in the United States bring guns to school. With that many weapons in the classroom, it is not surprising that an estimated 250,000 violent crimes are committed in U.S. high schools each month.[23] If some solution to the violence does not occur soon, these statistics will only increase. Consider these other disturbing reports:

In 1990, the U.S. Department of Health and Human Services reported that out of a sample of 11,631 ninth through twelfth graders, 4 percent admitted to carrying a gun at least once within the month prior to the survey. A 1987 survey of 11,000 eighth- and tenth-grade students in twenty states found that 3 percent of the males had brought a handgun to school during the year before the survey.[24]

STOPPING THE KILLING IN SCHOOLS

Schools can do much to prevent violence on their grounds, such as using metal detectors, increasing security, and emphasizing parent involvement. When kids wear their gang's colors, they stand out as members of that gang, making them easy targets for rival gang attacks. Thus, many schools are either outlawing the wearing of gang colors or requiring that school uniforms be worn, which eliminates wearing gang colors altogether.

In 1994, elementary and middle schools in Long Beach, California, began a mandatory school uniform policy—the first in the nation for an entire school district. The uniform requirement has contributed to a 36 percent drop in crime

As part of a drive to reduce gang violence, students at public schools in Long Beach, California, are required to wear school uniforms.

among elementary and middle school students.[25] Uniforms for students are freeing teachers to focus on teaching, and students to focus on learning. Test scores rose as students' schoolwork became more important than showing off what they were wearing, or resenting what someone else was wearing.

The success of the Long Beach school district has inspired school districts in other states to pass school uniform laws, including New York, Virginia, Georgia, Louisiana, and Maryland. In August 1995, California Governor Pete Wilson signed a bill requiring California school districts to implement a dress code.[26]

As school violence increases, schools are taking other measures to protect their students as well. For example, in many schools, armed security guards patrol the grounds. Metal detectors are becoming more and more common to keep kids from carrying weapons into school. And drug-sniffing dogs check out lockers for illegal substances. In addition, many schools are instituting antiviolence programs that teach kids peaceful ways of resolving conflicts.

It is becoming a tragic statement of the times when school administrators must ask for money for bulletproof glass instead of for books. If school violence is not stopped, and teachers start quitting in droves, the people who will suffer the most are kids. What will they do without teachers?

MURDER IN THE GANGS

On a spring day in April 1990, Ramon Rios was riding a bus in Los Angeles when suddenly he was shot and killed in front of fifteen other passengers. Ramon was killed because he was wearing all blue, the color worn by members of the Crips, a notorious East Los Angeles gang. Ramon's killers were members of a rival gang, the Bloods, who thought he belonged to the Crips. Ramon, however, did not belong to any gang.[27]

In 1991, a U.S. Department of Justice survey of law enforcement agencies found there were an estimated 5,000 gangs across the country. Total membership in these gangs was nearly 250,000. Gangs were responsible for an estimated 46,000 criminal incidents.[28] As of 1996, Los Angeles leads the country with 400 street gangs, composed of 60,000 members. In 1995, there were 408 gang-related murders in Los Angeles County.[29]

Teen gangs have been a major part of society since at least the 1830s. Charles Dickens wrote about such an early gang in his novel *Oliver Twist*: the villain Fagin's pack of young boys roaming the streets of London picking pockets.

In the twentieth-century United States, however, gangs have gone from petty lawbreaking to murder. And their territory has spread from the slums of the cities to the suburbs. Today's gangs conduct drug and weapons sales in schools, which for years had been considered "neutral turf." Gang activity in schools is the major cause of violence in classrooms today.

WHY KIDS JOIN GANGS

The main attraction of gangs to kids today is their ability to meet needs that are lacking in their lives—a sense of "fam ily" belonging and acceptance. With so many single-parent families and families torn apart by divorce and separation, kids do not have the traditional family support structure. They look for that support somewhere else, and they find it in the gang structure. Kids alienated from their families feel frustration and anger. Gang activity gives kids a sense of power and control and becomes an outlet for their anger.

Angela Southall, sixteen, Keane Flanell, twenty, and Ronice Williams, seventeen, used to go roller-skating every Tuesday, Saturday, and Sunday evening. They will not be roller-skating anymore. Early in the day on Saturday, January 28, 1996, gang members shot and killed a young girl on her own turf. In retaliation, members of the girl's gang decided to kill someone in the rival gang's neighborhood. That someone ended up being Angela Southall and her friends, none of whom were gang. members. They were standing in Angela's driveway, getting ready for their regular trip to the roller-skating rink.

Suddenly, a car drove by and fired a barrage of bullets at the three. "I heard a loud bang, bang, bang," said Angela's father. "My daughter was lying on her stomach. She said, 'Daddy, I got blood in my mouth.' She just went . . . on me." Within minutes, police found several suspects, including the alleged shooter.[30]

As this case illustrates, the majority of people killed in gang-related homicides are not gang members. They are usually innocent bystanders caught in the crossfire of drive-by shootings aimed at rival gang members over turf or drug clients, or in retaliation for murders of their members by rival gangs. Sometimes very young gang members even kill randomly as an initiation rite to join the gang.

Gang members carry guns the way most people carry their house keys. Consider this teenager's story: "There was a rival gang member, and we were shooting at each other. So, one day it ended up I was involved in a drive-by shooting. Which resulted in a death and an attempted murder. It just seemed fun. It gave me that acceptance that nobody else ever gave me in my family. That feeling was love. When I did a crime, they praised me. They'd say, 'Hey, right on. Good job, homey.'"[31]

FIGHTING BACK AGAINST GANG VIOLENCE

Experts agree that the best way to fight gang violence is to help kids at risk for gang recruitment *before* they join a gang. These kids can be given special assistance, such as peer counselors, mentors, academic tutoring, and classes in conflict resolution. Helping fulfill kids' needs that are not being met by their families is a way to keep kids from turning to gangs to fill those needs.

In Los Angeles, a program to keep kids out of gangs, called "L.A. Bridges," is scheduled to start in 1997. The program targets middle school children, the age when researchers say kids are most vulnerable to gangs. L.A. Bridges will fund nonprofit agencies to establish homework centers, parent-youth bonding programs, and conflict-resolution classes. Said Councilman Mike Hernandez, "You can't just take a gang member out of gangs. What you've got to do is replace the reasons they're in gangs. . . ."[32]

In addition, many cities have instituted curfews. For example, Atlanta has imposed an 11:00 P.M. curfew (midnight on weekends) for all teenagers under age sixteen. A California law has been passed that allows police to take into custody any youth under age eighteen who is on the streets after 1:00 A.M. Local police departments are also trying to discourage young people from joining gangs through workshops for kids and parents held in local schools.[33]

And one unlikely person is also doing his part to keep kids out of gangs. He is Stanley ("Tookie") Williams, who in 1971 co-founded the country's largest and most violent street gang, the Crips. Stanley, now forty-two, is on death row in California's San Quentin prison for the 1981 shotgunning of four people during motel and convenience store robberies. On death row he wrote and has had published the first half of a seventeen-book series titled *Tookie Speaks Out Against Gang Violence.* "You can learn from my mistakes," he says. "I apologize to you all for the atrocities which I and others committed through gang violence."[34]

Williams said that while in prison he realized the respect he cared so much about was based on intimidation, not self-respect. "Prevention is everything," he says. "By the time I was twelve, it was too late."[35] Williams has donated all money made from his book to inner-city help groups such as Mothers Against Gang Wars. "As much as you might want to fit in, don't join a gang," he writes in a section of his book called "Gangs and Wanting to Belong." "You won't find what you're looking for. All you will find is trouble, pain and sadness. I know. I did."[36]

In addition to getting tough on gangs, many experts on juvenile crime believe communities must also do something about the conditions that cause violent teen gangs to form in the first place, such as drug use and unemployment. "These kids don't care if they can be put in jail for the rest of their lives," says Carl Taylor, author of *Dangerous Society*, a study of Detroit gangs. "For many of them, life is already a jail. It's time for society to help unlock the cell."[37]

WILDING

In April 1989, at least a dozen boys stripped, raped, and beat a twenty-eight-year-old woman who was jogging in New York City's Central Park and left her for dead. A word was coined from this attack: *wilding*. Wilding is now used to mean a situation in which teenagers form a pack and roam around together, *going wild*—shooting, stabbing, slashing, robbing, or raping any available victim—solely for the "fun" of committing a crime.

On average, three such killings occur each year in New York City. The boys who attacked this woman were good students who came from middle-class homes with strict parents. When asked why they committed this crime, a fourteen-year-old suspect answered, "It was something to do. It was fun."[38]

Kids who commit wilding crimes feel they are only one kid in the middle of a mob. Therefore, they do not feel individually responsible for their crimes and feel no remorse. These criminals disregard their victims' pain and suffering. For example, just for "the fun of it," a mob of girls stormed the streets of upper Manhattan stabbing passersby with needles, hatpins, and scissors. In Missouri, three teenage boys wondered what it would be like to kill someone. They beat a classmate to death with baseball bats. And in Newark, New Jersey, a fight broke out among a mob of over 100 black and Hispanic teenagers in front of a pizzeria. A man tried to intervene but was attacked by the youths, including a seventeen-year-old who beat him to death with a golf club.[39]

•   •   •

Unless something is done to stop kids from killing in the neighborhoods, the death toll will keep rising. And if that happens, the words of this teenager will come true: "I'm frightened I might get shot in a drive-by. That's why I stay inside. . . . There's too much violence in the world. A bullet is waiting for me with my name on it. I know we got to die sometime, but I hope to die peaceful."[40]

FIVE

KIDS IN COURT

THE JUVENILE JUSTICE SYSTEM

TWELVE-YEAR-OLD BILLY was already due in court for armed robbery when he and two friends beat and raped a homeless woman in New York City's Central Park. When he was arrested, police discovered that a month earlier, Billy had murdered a woman in a similar rape and beating. At a hearing in Family Court, Billy received the maximum penalty a twelve-year-old could get: eighteen months at a juvenile boys' camp. After a year there, Billy was moved to a reentry program where he was allowed home for visits. On one visit, he disappeared.[1]

Billy's case is just one example of how the present juvenile justice system allows young offenders to get away with murder because they are children. Under adult law, murder is punishable with long jail sentences or the death penalty. But under juvenile law, murder is not called a crime but rather a "delinquent act." In many states, in fact, kids older than seven but under eighteen are not held criminally responsible for their acts, as they are presumed to be too young to understand the difference between right and wrong and to know the consequences of their actions. The current juvenile justice system assumes these kids can be rehabilitated and turned into productive citizens.

Critics of the system say juvenile laws were established in a different era, when delinquency meant truancy and petty theft. Today juvenile delinquents carry Uzis and murder people at random. These critics say that increasingly violent crimes by young offenders are a greater threat to public safety and thus should justify tougher punishments. They advocate the old saying that regardless of age, "If you do the crime, you do the time."

Pick any day of the year, and you will find more than 100,000 kids being held in juvenile facilities across the United States. The cost per year to keep a youth in a correctional center is $39,000, more than a year's tuition at America's most expensive colleges.[2] Every year, 2 million juveniles are arrested. Half of those are released due to inadequate evidence. In New York City in 1989 (the most recent year these statistics were compiled), 14,000 juveniles were arrested, but 42 percent never got prosecuted. Of those kids who did go to court, 70 percent were given suspended sentences or put on probation and released. On probation, juveniles are supposed to be monitored closely. Yet probation officers have huge caseloads and rarely have time to give in-depth attention to any one case. Therefore, most youths on probation go unsupervised.[3]

ROOTS OF THE AMERICAN JUVENILE JUSTICE SYSTEM

Until the nineteenth century in the United States, child criminals were tried as adults and given adult criminal sentences, including the death penalty. Reform of the juvenile justice system began at this time, when reformers pushed to institute rehabilitation for "wayward youths" instead of punishment. In the following years, a system of courts and laws developed to treat juveniles as special cases. In 1825, New York lawyer James W. Gerard led a movement to reform juvenile delinquents, arguing that child criminals forced to serve harsh sentences with adult criminals only fall deeper into a life of crime.[4]

REFORM SCHOOLS

As a result of Gerard's efforts to separate juvenile criminals from adult criminals, in 1825 the New York Society For The Reformation of Juvenile Delinquents opened America's first juvenile reformatory, named the House of Refuge, in New York City. The school attempted to reform delinquents through prayer, work, and study, carried out almost entirely in silence. Still, the teachers often resorted to beatings, solitary confinement, and leg irons.[5]

By the mid-nineteenth century, other juvenile institutions were established across the country. Reformers experimented with different ways to rehabilitate juvenile offenders. For example, the Boston House of Reformation, founded in 1826, put some inmates in charge of disciplining their peers. In 1854, the Children's Aid Society of New York took young vagrants out of urban gangs and placed them with rural families. The Massachusetts State Reform School for Girls pioneered the "family system" in 1855, which created small groups of girls living together under the guidance of a supervisor.

These new approaches, however, often punished kids who had not committed any crimes. Judges often put children in reform schools for behavior problems such as "idleness, incorrigibility, mischievous propensities, or associating with vicious persons." In addition, parents could commit their children without a reason.[6]

THE FIRST JUVENILE COURTS

In 1899, Judge Benjamin Lindsey of Denver, Colorado, visited the home of an immigrant boy he had sent to reform school for stealing coal. He found the family in such poverty that he realized the boy had not stolen because he was a criminal. Rather, his horrible living conditions had caused him to steal to survive. Judge Lindsey's philosophy of looking deeper than the criminal act itself in sentencing juveniles became the cornerstone of the current juvenile justice system.

That same year, Cook County, Illinois, opened the first juvenile court. The court's goal was to rehabilitate juveniles with treatment and supervision, in effect becoming a substitute parent, saving kids from negative influences that lead to crime. By 1925, juvenile courts were operating in forty-six states.[7] In keeping with Judge Lindsey's philosophy, the court held hearings instead of trials and sent offenders to training schools instead of prison. The system viewed violent juvenile criminals as children who happened to commit crimes, rather than as criminals who happened to be young.[8]

COMMUNITY-BASED JUVENILE FACILITIES

By the 1970s, that viewpoint began to change. State reform schools had become so overcrowded and understaffed that criminologists found the schools were in effect functioning as training grounds for kids to become hardened criminals once released. In 1972, Massachusetts closed all five of its reform schools. Jailed youths were paroled, placed in group homes, or turned over to privately run, community-based programs. The new system worked so much better than traditional reform schools that in 1974, Congress passed laws encouraging all states to close their reform schools.[9]

By 1977, many juvenile courts redesigned themselves in the mold of adult courts. The state of Washington introduced sentences linked to the severity of the crime. A year later, New York passed a law directing that thirteen-year-olds charged with murder be tried in criminal courts. And in 1986, the U.S. Justice Department recommended states adopt standard penalties for juvenile criminals. Previously, juvenile courts had looked at offenders' personal histories, not their crimes, to determine sentences. Thus, two juveniles charged with the same crime could receive very different sentences. And in 1989, the U.S. Supreme Court upheld the death penalty for convicted sixteen-year-olds.[10]

THE MODERN JUVENILE JUSTICE SYSTEM

Today's juvenile justice system is overwhelmed with the Yummy Sandfords and Eric Smiths of the world. Studies show that 30 percent to 40 percent of all boys growing up in urban areas of the United States are arrested before their eighteenth birthday. About 10 percent of them will be arrested again. Said Judge Susan R. Winfield of the Family Division of the Washington, D.C., Superior Court, "Youngsters used to shoot each other in the body. Then in the head. Now they shoot each other in the face."[11]

Because of the outcry against current juvenile laws, criminologists are turning their attention toward changing the juvenile justice system. They are faced with a dilemma, however, because they question both the helpfulness of short prison sentences given to kids who kill and the benefit of putting kids in adult prisons for long sentences, where they live with hardened, adult murderers. They suggest that prosecuting kids as adults serves not to rehabilitate but rather to further reinforce their criminal behavior.

The rising juvenile crime rate affects all classes of society. Clyde Crohnkhite, deputy police chief of the Los Angeles Police Department, did a study to find common denominators between juvenile criminals from well-to-do and from economically deprived homes. He found both sets of children had low self-esteem, no strong parental supervision, believed they were not important to their parents, and had no purpose in society. Both sets of juvenile offenders said no one was home when they returned from school, so they had no one to complain to or brag about their day.[12]

When children are tried as juveniles, they are rarely photographed or fingerprinted; their hearings are private, their sentences lenient; and their records are kept secret and later destroyed, so no criminal record trails them into adulthood. In most states, when juveniles are found guilty, they are sentenced to a juvenile lockup facility until their twenty-fifth birthday. Critics say this punishment amounts to no more than a slap on the wrist.

CHANGING THE SYSTEM: TRYING KIDS AS ADULTS

How should the legal system treat children who commit acts that, until recently, were committed only by hard-core criminal adults? Los Angeles District Attorney Gil Garcetti said, "We need to throw out our entire juvenile justice system. We should replace it with one that both protects society from violent juvenile criminals and efficiently rehabilitates youths who can be saved—and can differentiate between the two."[13]

In most states, juveniles under age seven are considered

not responsible for their criminal acts, including homicide. These children may not be prosecuted at all, even for murder. One remedy has been to lower the age at which juveniles charged with serious crimes—murder, rape, and armed assault—can be tried in adult courts. The idea is if these kids are tried as adults, they will get jail time, a "real" punishment. In Dade County, Florida, for example, more kids are tried in adult court than in any other American county—almost 600 kids in 1994.[14]

Other states are following suit. Colorado permits fourteen- to seventeen-year-olds to be tried as adults in cases of violent crime. In January 1994, California, which has the highest juvenile incarceration rate in the country, lowered from sixteen to fourteen the age at which juveniles can be tried as adults. Although youths under eighteen in California cannot be given the death penalty, those fourteen and older can be given life in prison without the possibility of parole. Georgia allows juveniles ages fourteen through seventeen to be automatically tried as adults. In Connecticut, New York, North Carolina, and Vermont, juveniles are automatically tried as adults at age sixteen.[15]

Critics complain that trying kids as adults is not the answer to rising juvenile crime, as so many of these kids go right back to committing crimes as soon as they are out of prison. These critics cite California, where new, get-tough policies had no effect on deterring juvenile crime. After spending fourteen months or more in a state institution, 70 percent of California youths were rearrested after their release.[16]

WHEN JUVENILES ARE TRIED AS ADULTS

The decision to try a minor as an adult is made by a judge, who must take certain factors into account as specified by the United States Supreme Court in its 1966 decision *Kent v. United States.* According to those criteria, juvenile offenders can be tried as adults only if they have reached their teens; have been charged with either murder, manslaughter, rape, kidnapping, armed robbery, arson, sodomy, or aggravated assault; and have been found by mental health professionals to be dangerous and unable to be rehabilitated in the juvenile justice system.[17]

Dr. Joel Peter Eigen, a sociologist, found that juvenile killers who met any of the following four criteria were especially likely to be tried as adults: (1) they killed during the commission of a felony, (2) they were at least seventeen at the time of the killing, (3) the juvenile was the main assailant, and (4) they had a prior criminal record.[18]

THE CASE OF ANDRE GREEN

On July 27, 1994, a young woman phoned 911 from her apartment near Raleigh, North Carolina, to beg for help. Just before the phone went dead, she was heard screaming, "Don't harm my baby!" Over the next several minutes, she was beaten bloody with a mop handle and raped. The attacker was a neighbor who had become infatuated with her. The woman was twenty-two; her rapist was thirteen.

He was Andre Green, who was the first juvenile tried under a 1994 North Carolina law permitting children as young as thirteen to be tried as adults. Green, who was sentenced to twenty-five years to life, will not be eligible for parole for twenty years. Frank Jackson, head of the Dangerous Offenders Task Force in Wake County, North Carolina, fears that such a long prison term may make Green worse. "It's kind of scary to think what kind of monster may be created," Jackson says. "He could be released at the age of thirty-three, after having been raised with some of the most hardened criminals North Carolina has to offer."[19]

THE CASE OF TONY HICKS

In San Diego, California, the youngest person ever charged with murder in California, and the first person to fall under the new law lowering the age at which an accused murderer can be tried as an adult, was Tony Hicks, age fourteen. He was convicted of the January 21, 1995, murder of Tariq Khamisa, twenty, a college student and pizza deliveryman. Hicks shot Khamisa point-blank with a 9-mm semiautomatic handgun after Khamisa refused to give up his cash or pizza.

Tony Hicks was sentenced to twenty-five years to life. Upon hearing his sentence, he tearfully told the judge, "I'll be a better person. I won't mess up. I want to hold my mom as tight as I can and beg her to take me out of jail."[20] He will spend ten years in a California Youth Authority facility before being transferred to state prison. He will not be eligible for parole until he is thirty-six.

Tony Hicks is a perfect example of a kid whose life was characterized by almost all the ingredients that experts say go into making a kid who kills. He grew up with violence in his home. He was beaten by his parents, who lived in South Central Los Angeles. His father served time in prison. Hicks had moved to San Diego to live with his grandfather, but ran away just weeks before he murdered Khamisa. Along with Hicks, three accomplices were also convicted. Two fourteen-year-olds were tried in juvenile court, and the eighteen-year-old who organized the robbery and ordered Hicks to shoot was tried in adult court and sentenced to life in prison without parole. The boys had spent the night drinking alcohol and smoking marijuana before they decided to lure a pizza deliveryman to a phony address and rob him.[21]

PROBLEMS WITH THE
MODERN JUVENILE JUSTICE SYSTEM

An agreement among criminologists is emerging that the juvenile justice system takes forever to punish kids who seriously break the law, and it devotes far too much time and money to hardened young criminals, while neglecting at-risk kids who could still be turned around. "We can't look a kid in the eye and tell him that we can't spend a thousand dollars on him when he's twelve or thirteen, but that we'll be glad to reserve a jail cell for him and spend a hundred grand a year on him later," says North Carolina Attorney General Mike Easley.[22]

In addition, seasoned juvenile criminals have gone through the juvenile justice system many times. Therefore, they know exactly how much time they have to serve for each kind of crime and are not afraid of getting caught for a crime they know will get them only a few months to a year in a juvenile lockup. A question raised by a teenage boy to Los Angeles District Attorney Gil Garcetti at a juvenile detention center sums up the attitude of experienced kid criminals: "Right now, I'm under sixteen. If I kill someone, I get out of prison when I'm twenty-five, right?"[23]

Another seventeen-year-old, in a lockup for grand theft auto and aggravated assault, raises another problem. Prison does not last forever, and life on the outside is an open invitation to go bad again. As he says, "They send you straight back into the same situation. The house is dirty when you left it, and it's dirty when you get back."[24]

Critics of the new laws trying kids as adults say such youths commit even more crimes after release than do those who remain in the juvenile system. Says criminology professor Charles Frazier of the University of Florida, trying a youth as an adult may "stigmatize him as a lost cause and convince him he is no good," resulting in a return to crime.[25] Mr. Frazier's point is backed up in Jacksonville, Florida, at least. There, kids tried as adults are incarcerated in local jails that offer education and treatment programs. The result? Juvenile crime in Jacksonville has dropped.[26]

PUNISHING KIDS WHO KILL

When a child is arrested for the first time and the crime is a misdemeanor, he or she may be assigned community work and avoid appearing in juvenile court at all. In many states, community work takes the form of *restitution*, in which the child reimburses the victim either through direct payment or through some form of public service.

The problem is what happens after the child is arrested a second time. Most states have a severe shortage of residential programs, in which kids receive psychological and vocational counseling. Therefore, some juveniles go into locked facilities without the much needed mental health counseling, while other kids are sent to a psychiatric setting within the state mental health system, which is not geared to the problems of juvenile offenders. Moreover, many of the juvenile residential programs that do exist are not secure. Escapes occur daily.

When juveniles are prosecuted a second time, most of them are either put on probation or sentenced to another six months in jail and then released to the street, carrying with them the same problems they had before serving time.[27] Says Los Angeles County juvenile court judge Roosevelt Dorn, "We repeatedly send these young lawbreakers home with a slap on the wrist, until they finally commit horrendous crimes because no one has put the brakes on them. We program these children for failure."[28]

BACK ON THE STREETS, BACK IN JAIL

In many inner-city neighborhoods, kids view prison time more as a rite of passage than as a punishment. "Their father's been in prison; their brother's been in prison," says Lieutenant Robert Losacka, a Texas prison guard. "It's part of growing up. Once back on the street, these youths enjoy enhanced social status." Adds Paul Cromwell, a University of Miami criminologist, "Prison systems create criminals."[29]

James Woodley, who since the age of nineteen has been arrested fourteen times on felonies ranging from burglary to selling cocaine, agrees. "Jail suited me just fine," he says. "You get healthy. You eat good, you sleep good, you get cable TV. Then you get out. They don't teach you anything. So guys come out and do the same thing all over again."[30] These "revolving door" criminals explain why 80 percent of all crimes are committed by about 20 percent of the criminals.

Professor Ira Schwartz, director of the Center For The Study of Youth Policy at the University of Michigan at Ann Arbor, says the only hope for stopping juvenile homicide is to attack the roots of juvenile crime: poverty, deteriorating education systems, rampant drug use, child abuse, and neglect. He says, "Until we realize we need every child in this country to be healthy, well-fed, and educated, we're heading in the wrong direction."[31]

KILLING KIDS WHO KILL

While the death penalty is rarely given as a sentence, and even more rarely carried out in the United States, our nation is one of the few that allow the execution of individuals for crimes committed while they were juveniles. Since 1979, Amnesty International has documented only eight executions of juveniles in the world, three of those in the United States.

Thirty-seven states permit capital punishment. Twelve of these states (California, Colorado, Connecticut, Illinois, Maryland, Nebraska, New Jersey, New Hampshire, New Mexico, Ohio, Oregon, and Tennessee) prohibit capital punishment for crimes committed before age eighteen. Three others (Georgia, North Carolina, and Texas) forbid execution of juveniles for crimes committed before age seventeen. Twenty-two states allow the execution of juveniles for murders committed before they were seventeen.[32]

On January 23, 1983, fifteen-year-old William Wayne Thompson beat, stabbed, and shot to death Charles Keene, his former brother-in-law, in retaliation for Keene's abuse of William's sister. He was tried as an adult for first-degree murder, convicted, and sentenced to die. The case was appealed, and in 1988 the Supreme Court ruled that executing a fifteen-year-old would amount to cruel and unusual punishment, and therefore violate the Eighth Amendment to the U.S. Constitution. This ruling effectively established age sixteen as the official minimum age at which juveniles could be executed in the United States for those states that did not have a minimum age written into their laws.[33]

STANFORD V. KENTUCKY

The Supreme Court upheld that decision in 1989 in two cases decided together: *Stanford* v. *Kentucky* and *Wilkins* v. *Missouri*. This time the question before the Court was whether the Eighth Amendment could be applied to executing individuals for crimes they committed while sixteen or seventeen years old. Keven Stanford was seventeen when he robbed a

Kentucky gas station, raped the female attendant, then shot her point-blank in the face and head. Heath Wilkins was sixteen when he robbed a convenience store, stabbed the female cashier, then left her lying on the floor to die.

Both Kevin Stanford and Heath Wilkins were tried as adults, convicted of first-degree murder, and sentenced to die. In a five to four decision, the Supreme Court found it to be constitutionally correct to execute sixteen- and seventeen-year-olds for murder, and even younger kids if lawmakers of a state had fully debated the issue and set a minimum age for the death penalty. Thus, Heath Wilkins and Kevin Stanford remain on death row awaiting their executions.[34]

KIDS SENTENCED TO DEATH: "CHUCKIE"

Between January 1, 1973, and December 31, 1993, there were nine executions of men who were juveniles when sentenced to death. Charles Rumbaugh, nicknamed "Chuckie," was one. He committed his first burglary at age six. Between ages thirteen and twenty-eight, Chuckie spent all but eight months in reform schools, mental hospitals, and prisons. He was seventeen when he shot and killed a Texas jeweler during a robbery in 1974. He was convicted in 1975 and given the death penalty. On September 11, 1985, Charles Rumbaugh was executed by lethal injection, after spending ten years on death row. Chuckie Rumbaugh's execution made headlines across the country for being the first time in two decades that a person was put to death in the United States for a crime committed while he was a juvenile.[35]

KIDS SENTENCED TO DEATH: TERRY ROACH

James Terry Roach of South Carolina was seventeen when he pleaded guilty to the rape and murder of a fourteen-year-old girl and her seventeen-year-old boyfriend. Shortly before the murders, Roach, borderline mentally retarded, ran away from reform school. He and two friends, one sixteen and the other twenty-two, were high on alcohol and drugs in October 1977 when they went driving around "looking for a girl to rape." They found a couple sitting in a car near a baseball diamond. Roach shot the boy in the head, then dragged the girl out of the car. The three boys raped her, then Roach and the younger boy shot her five times in the head.

The younger boy turned state's evidence to avoid the death penalty. The older man was executed in 1985. After spending nine years on death row, Terry Roach was put to death in the South Carolina electric chair on January 10, 1986.[36]

KIDS SENTENCED TO DEATH: JAY KELLY PINKERTON

Jay Kelly Pinkerton was twice sentenced to die. He was seventeen in 1979 when he raped, murdered, and then mutilated an Amarillo, Texas, housewife as her children lay sleeping in another room. His second conviction resulted from a 1980 sex slaying in which he raped another Amarillo woman in a furniture store, then stabbed her over thirty times. He was convicted of the two murders and given the death penalty. On May 15, 1986, six years later, Pinkerton was executed in the Texas electric chair.[37]

PROS AND CONS OF THE DEATH PENALTY

Those in favor of the death penalty for minors believe that kids can distinguish between right and wrong and should suffer the consequences of their acts. In addition, they believe the death penalty would decrease teenage violence. Those opposed to the death penalty for minors say the line should be drawn at age eighteen, usually considered the beginning of adulthood. A sixteen- or seventeen-year-old, experts say, is still maturing emotionally and intellectually. If society considers these teens too young to vote, drink, or join the armed forces, how, they ask, can they be seen as adults when it comes to crime? And finally, many juvenile crime experts believe young people have a better chance at rehabilitation than adults.

Consider the case of Paula Cooper. At age fifteen, she was convicted of brutally murdering an eighty-five-year-old Bible teacher. Now twenty-six, she is serving a life prison sentence. But since arriving in prison, Paula has completed her high school equivalency exam and taken college correspondence courses. She says she wants to help keep other kids from making the same mistakes she did.[38]

REFORMING TODAY'S JUVENILE JUSTICE SYSTEM

Attorneys, judges, and others in the justice system agree that America's juvenile justice system is outdated, inadequate, and no longer able to cope with the violence committed by kids. A system designed to deal with runaway children, truants, and young shoplifters is now being flooded with young killers.

University of Southern California criminologist James Q. Wilson believes punishment should begin very young, with small sentences that are escalated over time, as the repetition and the severity of the offenses continue. "Punishment works best when it's close to the act," he says.[39] Marcus Felson, a UCLA sociology professor, agrees, saying, "An electric plug that shocks you a year later, or once in a thousand times, isn't going to deter you from touching the plug."[40]

L.A. County judge Roosevelt Dorn agrees and believes in catching these kids in the court's net as soon as they take their first missteps and monitoring them until they realize an education and a productive life are more rewarding than causing death by gang-banging. He believes the only way the courts will know kids are complying with their probation conditions is by calling them back to court frequently to see how they are doing. Judge Dorn says when a kid is put on probation without requiring him to appear in court again, the kid knows that as long as he does not get caught he can keep committing crimes.

Adds Judge David B. Mitchell of the Baltimore, Maryland, Circuit Court, "It's of no value to work miracles in rehabilitation if children return to the same squalor from which they came. In America, there is an underclass of poor kids who can see the other side through the glass, but don't know how to get there. Until we solve this problem, we're going to have kids who kill."[41]

SIX

STOPPING
KIDS WHO KILL

ONE NIGHT IN 1994, fifteen-year-old Alex Casillas heard screams coming from the house next door. When he ran outside, he saw his best friend, Albert Diaz, lying in his yard, bleeding from gunshot wounds. Albert was wounded too badly to live, so his friends had brought him home to die. In doing so, they saved Alex Casillas's life.

"I saw him lying there," Alex said, "and I thought, 'I don't wanna end up like that.'"[1] He didn't. Today Alex is getting good grades and plays on the basketball team of his high school. But he was heading down the road to an early grave or prison when Albert was killed. Although he had not joined a gang at the time, he wore baggy, gang-style clothes, smoked marijuana, drank excessively, and had been kicked out of five schools. His mother struggled with him constantly not to join a gang.

After Albert was killed, Alex started talking to Raul Caiz, director of the El Sereno Youth Center. Raul made Alex realize gang life was not for him. Today Alex wants to become a youth counselor like Raul and steer troubled kids away from the life he came so close to living.[2]

.   .   .

The efforts of his mother and Raul Caiz helped stop Alex Casillas from killing. But what about kids who do not have a mother like Mrs. Casillas or do not know a director of a youth center? What can be done to stop today's delinquents before they become tomorrow's murderers? And what can be done so that kids who do kill will not kill again?

THE THREE-STRIKES LAW

A Senate crime bill calls for a national "three-strikes" law, meaning a person who commits three felonies is automatically sentenced to life in prison—that criminal is *out* of society for good. The state of Washington already has such a law, and at least thirty other states are considering the idea. Many police officers, prosecutors, and judges, however, claim the three-strikes law will have little impact on crime, as most felons are not convicted a third time until late in their crime careers.

Many citizens agree, questioning whether filling up jails with teenagers is the answer to stopping kids from killing. Some experts argue that a better way to divert kids from a life of crime is a rehabilitation program that gets juvenile offenders off the streets and offers them intensive educational tutoring and counseling, psychotherapy, and mentors who help them pursue a productive life.[3]

CRIME PREVENTION PROGRAMS

With so many kids going right back to a life of crime after they get out of juvenile facilities, many police officers, judges, and others in law enforcement are pushing for a greater emphasis on *prevention* instead of punishment. For example, the police department in Long Beach, California, launched a prevention program to reward children for good behavior. Said police corporal Harry Erickson, "You know how we normally give out tickets for bad behavior; we now give kids tickets for good behavior. If we see a kid following safety laws, such as wearing his bicycle helmet, we give him a ticket to appear for a free ice cream cone or a free pizza."[4]

Besides police departments, other areas of society as well are forming coalitions to prevent youth violence. These areas include schools, hospitals, universities, youth organizations, churches, the YMCA, and other nonprofit organizations. The belief is that at-risk children can be identified as early as the first or second grade. Intensive educational, counseling, and personal contact with such kids by caring adults can help at-risk kids make the right choices to stay out of trouble. Who exactly are at-risk kids? Experts on juvenile crime have discovered indicators that certain kids will likely become juvenile offenders: poor grades, truancy, classroom misbehavior, gang affiliation, and alcohol or drug use.[5]

California has begun several coalition programs. One is a "First Offender Program," in which children ages eight to eighteen who have been arrested for the first time participate, along with their parents, in counseling sessions aimed at keeping the child in school. Every Friday, the children talk about taking responsibility for their actions and participate in recreational activities. A probation officer visits the child's school once a week to make sure he or she is attending classes, and also helps find tutors and mentors for the child. The program is a joint operation of the YMCA, Los Angeles County Probation Department, and the Cambodian Association of America.[6]

INTERVENTION PROGRAMS

Another kind of program attacking juvenile crime through prevention is the intervention program. Designed to recreate a sense of family, interventions attempt to step into the lives of children who are *at risk* to commit crimes but have not yet done so, in order to help them get off the road to crime. Interventions for at-risk kids provide tutoring, after-school activities, and counseling. Interventions are intense, with everyday contact and follow-up.

In an intervention project in New York City, for example, some of the poorest teenagers participate in small, after-school arts workshops or other youth programs where they bond with adults and work on personal goals. David Saltzman of the Robin Hood Foundation, which funds the project, says, "The key is finding adults who will give the kids what your parents gave you: love, discipline, attention, the ability to fail and still be cared about."[7]

In Long Beach, California, children between the ages of eight and fourteen who fit the at-risk profile are matched up with organizations like the YMCA, the Boy and Girl Scouts, or other community organizations. Members of these organizations provide tutoring, family counseling, and other intervention services.[8]

There is also a national intervention program, AmeriCorps, sponsored by the Clinton administration. AmeriCorps attempts to find young adults willing to make an intensive commitment to at-risk kids. AmeriCorps workers spend thirty minutes with each kid every day and pay weekly home visits to get parents involved. Says director Michael Houston, "If you have someone there telling them every day 'I know you can do this'—then eventually it happens."[9]

MENTORING PROGRAMS

A variation on intervention programs is mentoring programs, which like the AmeriCorps program, uses specially trained adults who try to become role models for inner-city kids. These adults, called mentors, spend time with the kids, to help them see there can be a good life for them if they stay out of gangs and away from violence and crime. California started the California Mentor Initiative to recruit 250,000 role models for at-risk kids. Volunteers are trained by a counseling and crisis service called Family Helpline.

David Kobrin, a teacher's assistant in his everyday life, has been serving as a mentor to twelve-year-old Kenneth Smith, a South Central Los Angeles boy who lives with his grandparents, four siblings, and three cousins. During the first year of David's mentoring, Kenneth made his first A in his schoolwork, and did things few South Central kids ever do—he went whale watching on a boat, rode in the cockpit of a jet, and witnessed a taping of the TV show *Family Matters*. David meets with Kenneth once a week for an hour to talk or review homework. The outings occur anywhere from one to several times a month. David has developed a nurturing, trusting friendship with Kenneth, who looks up to him and eagerly awaits each visit—which is what mentoring is really all about.[10]

COLORADO'S YOUTH OFFENDER SYSTEM

After a deadly juvenile crime wave in 1993, Colorado established its Youth Offender System (YOS). Kids between fourteen and eighteen who have been convicted of felonies in adult court can have their sentences suspended in exchange for spending two to six years in the 300-bed YOS fa-

A troubled teen undergoes the rigors of a military-style
mini-boot camp in Colorado's experimental Youth Offender System.

cility in Pueblo. A YOS term begins with a month of military-style boot camp to break down tough-guy attitudes and teach respect for adult authority. Next comes a program of personalized counseling and education, lasting anywhere from eight months to five years. Academic subjects are mixed with computer literacy and vocational training, to help kids earn high school equivalency diplomas and prepare for careers.

Classroom studies are followed by a prerelease phase of three months of life skills training and planning for how the teen will make it on the outside. Following release, the juvenile goes through six to twelve months of intensive supervision, involving frequent reporting to parole officers, electronic monitoring, random urinalysis (to test for drug use), and involvement in community support programs. Kids who get into trouble can be put back into the YOS for another term. Then if they wash out of YOS a second time, their original suspended sentences can be reapplied.[11]

Variations on Colorado's approach to young offenders can be found throughout the country. In Bridgeport, Connecticut, for example, the Powerline Intensive Youth Center gives kids an alternative to prison. Teenagers attend academic classes for up to nine months, learn computer skills, and learn how to find a job. In Du Page County, Illinois, outside Chicago, the Sheriff's Work Alternative Program has been extended to juveniles, sending them out on community service jobs, such as painting and cleaning streets and parks.[12]

BOOT CAMPS

Some states are experimenting with jail boot camps as a first step in rehabilitating juvenile offenders who are not yet firmly committed to a life of crime. The ultimate goal of these programs is rehabilitation of such kids through exposure to educational and employment opportunities. Also called "shock incarceration," this alternative to jail sends first-time, nonviolent juvenile offenders to a military-style camp, similar to an army basic training facility, for three to six months. Jail boot camps feature military drills, hard labor, substance abuse treatment, counseling, and educational and vocational training.

Boot camps seek to instill in these kids discipline, routine, and unquestioning obedience to orders, to help them develop law-abiding values and prepare them to obtain future employment. As the offender progresses through the program, boot camps allow a gradual shifting from hard labor to education and community service. Privileges also increase as an inmate's performance progresses. For example, neither TV nor visits by friends or relatives are allowed for the first thirty days.[13]

Camp Falcon in Golden, Colorado, is one such boot camp. Boys from Colorado are sent there by judges who demand completion of the program as part of their probation. Military-style discipline includes shaved heads, making beds without creases, standing erect in food lines, and speaking only when spoken to. "The first minute we get them, we explain who we are," said Technical Sergeant Chuck Isner, the camp's program manager. "We care about them . . . and are going to be there for them. We promise we are not going to go away. We tell them they will succeed."[14] Isner believes the program will succeed, too, as these boys have not spent years being on the wrong side of the law. In addition, the juvenile prison next door is a constant reminder of the fate that awaits them if they do not pass muster in boot camp.

PRISON SCHOOLS

The Lloyd McCorkle Training School in Skillman, New Jersey, looks like a typical high school. But McCorkle's student body is not typical. They are juvenile delinquents, and the school is in reality a prison for young offenders. Boys and girls between the ages of thirteen and seventeen, who are serving sentences from six months to two years, attend regular classes and after-school activities such as graphic arts, football, and basketball. But the classroom doors are locked from the outside and guarded by officers. And no one goes home after school. The academic program is state-accredited, which means kids get credit for classes they pass. This credit can be applied toward a diploma at their own high school.

Inmates live in cottages that sleep twenty and are guarded around the clock. The daily regimen includes strict discipline and positive reinforcement. Troublemakers are given extra cleaning duties, such as floor buffing or toilet scrubbing, or are barred from receiving visitors or attending Friday night movies. Inmates who become violent are locked up for a day in one of the cells at the far end of the compound. Repeat offenders are shipped out to more secure facilities. Beth Robbins, director of education, says, "A lot of these kids have been abused all of their lives. They have no self-esteem; they think they're nobody. We might be the first people in their lives to actually do what we say we'll do."[15]

Programs designed to foster self-worth include morning meetings in small groups to talk about participants' problems. The staff encourages inmates to solve their problems themselves. On the streets, these kids handled problems with violence. At McCorkle, they learn to handle conflicts by talking. Good behavior is rewarded with lightened sentences and expanded privileges, including weekend visits home, outings, vocational classes at a nearby technical school, and part-time jobs.[16]

VICTIM AWARENESS PROGRAMS

Many juvenile lockups offer Victim Awareness classes, where students role-play the crimes they have committed, taking the part of their victim. In this way, they learn to feel the pain they inflicted on their victim, and thus feel empathy for their victim and remorse for their crime. When these kids are released, they stand a better chance of not committing crimes again.

One inmate said about the Victim Awareness program, "This class has made me feel the pain I was lashing out on other people. I could have walked up to you and blown your brains out because I didn't feel. But once you really feel what you've done was wrong, it's hard to repeat it."[17]

CURFEWS

Another tool to control crime before it happens is teen curfews. Tampa, Florida, for example, adopted a curfew for kids sixteen or younger: 11:00 P.M. on weeknights, midnight on weekends. It is the parents who get punished if their child violates the curfew. Parents get away with a warning the first time; the next time, the penalty can consist of a $1,000 fine, six months in jail, or fifty hours of community service. In New Orleans, Louisiana, violent youth crime fell 27 percent after a dusk-to-dawn curfew went into effect for those under age eighteen.[18]

KIDS DO THE CRIME, PARENTS DO THE TIME

Lawmakers in several states are trying to force parents to take control of their children's behavior by passing laws to make them more accountable for their children's acts. For example, in 1988, California passed an antigang law allowing police to arrest parents for failure to exercise reasonable care, supervision, protection, and control over their minor child. In 1989, Florida passed a law subjecting parents and any other gun-owning adults to a five-year prison term and a $5,000 fine if a child uses a gun that has been left around the house. In 1995, ten states enacted laws imposing penalties, from counseling to fines and jail time, against parents whose children commit crimes.[19]

The first parents tried under the new laws were the Provenzino couple of St. Clair Shores, Michigan. In May 1995, their sixteen-year-old son, Alex, was questioned by police in connection with three church burglaries. He was let go, but police warned his father, Anthony, to take control of his son. The next month, Alex attacked his father with a golf club during an argument. His father phoned police, who arrested Alex and placed him in a youth home. He was there for only one night, as his parents did not want him in the same place as "murderers and rapists."[20]

Over the next weeks, Alex robbed several homes, stashing the loot in his room. His parents grew more and more afraid for their safety and that of their two younger daughters. In September, Alex was charged with burglary and weapons and drug possession. This time, the Provenzinos did not fight the police's decision to return Alex to a youth home during the trial. Two months later, he was sentenced to one year in juvenile detention.

In May 1996, the Provenzinos were put on trial themselves. A city attorney asked them why they had supported Alex's release from juvenile custody, why they had not sought counseling for him, and if they felt any responsibility for Alex's crimes. "I feel partly to blame," his mother said. "But I do not feel as though I was negligent as a mother."[21]

The six-member jury felt otherwise. They convicted the Provenzinos of violating the city ordinance that requires parents to exercise reasonable control over their minor children. The Provenzinos were fined $100 each and ordered to pay $2,000 in court costs. Their penalty was relatively low —they could have been given up to $27,000 in fines and court costs.

While many citizens applaud the new parental laws, other experts say the laws are unconstitutional. Professor Martin Guggenheim, a specialist in juvenile law at New York University School of Law, says, "We are each responsible for ourselves under the criminal law—it's not guilt by association."[22] The Provenzinos and other families in their situation would most likely agree.

Critics also point out that by the time kids reach the age at which they become criminal problems, parents already have less control over them and thus little chance of taking control of their kids' behavior. They believe jailing parents only worsens the problem of prison overcrowding and further destabilizes the family unit by leaving kids without parents.

IT TAKES AN ENTIRE VILLAGE

The psychological impact of witnessing violence can be as devastating to children as if they themselves had been assaulted. Research has shown that kids who suffer the harshest treatment at home are more likely to treat their playmates violently. As adults, they are more likely to abuse their own children. Therefore, early help is crucial for kids who experience family violence. There is a well-known expression, "It takes an entire village to raise a child."

To Angela Blackwell, director of the Black Community Crusade for Children, a national effort to help inner-city kids, this means filling children's lives with many caring adults. "Young people are afraid," she says. "They're afraid to go to parties, to sporting events, or just a walk to and from school. One of the things fear does to children is they fail to develop close relationships with multiple people. So they fail to learn to trust."[23]

The Black Community Crusade attempts to reach out to these children by providing people in schools, churches, and neighborhood organizations to listen to them and help guide them when their own parents are either not available or unwilling to listen. The Crusade finds a house where adults gather and makes it known that children with problems are welcome to come there.

MAD DADS

In 1989, a father upset over a gang attack on his son held a meeting in a church basement in Omaha, Nebraska, with seven other African-American fathers. The men, fed up with drugs in their neighborhood, founded "Mad Dads." Not only do organization members patrol streets after midnight to chase drug dealers away from the neighborhood, but they also find drug prevention and gang intervention programs for kids in trouble. They also attempt to become surrogate fathers to kids growing up in households without a male role model. In addition, Mad Dads escorts kids who have had problems with gang members to and from school. They carry cellular phones and cards with a phone number to call. They tell the kids if you phone this number, you will connect with an adult who cares about you.[24]

Mad Dads has been so successful in keeping kids off the streets and off drugs that it now has 25,000 members in fourteen states.[25] One such program is Fort Worth, Texas's "Texas's Citizens on Patrol." More than 1,000 civilians have taken a twelve-hour law-enforcement course, then volunteered as auxiliary police. In 1986, Fort Worth led the FBI's list of most crime-ridden cities. In 1994, it was the twelfth on the list, with crime down 50 percent.[26]

SOBRIETY HIGH

Fact: Most kids who attend high school today will be exposed to drugs; any kid who gets involved in drugs will be exposed to violence; and any kid who is high on drugs has a higher chance of committing violence, especially murder.[27]

One city decided to do something about this fact. In a suburb of Minneapolis, Minnesota, is Sobriety High, the only school in the United States devoted exclusively to teenagers in recovery from drug and alcohol abuse. The school, which accepts only forty-five students on a first-come first-served basis, is for students who have completed drug and alcohol rehabilitation and do not want to return to their regular school. When most kids complete a rehab program, they go back to the same school, with the same kids dealing and using drugs and alcohol. They have no skills to resist getting hooked again.

One of the four teachers at Sobriety says, "These kids need a safe environment where they can walk in the door and nobody is going to say, 'Want to smoke a joint? Want to share a bag?'"[28] Funded by the state of Minnesota, the school is free. Each student must sign a contract to remain sober. Three relapses and you're out. In addition, each student must participate in an hour of group therapy every day. In the group, they have an opportunity to talk about what is going on in their lives. They get help dealing with drug-related issues, such as staying sober while living in a home in which other family members use drugs.

Jay, a student at Sobriety, said, "If I went back to a public school, where I know all the people that use there, there's no way I could walk around the school and say *no* all day long."[29] Another student, Janel, said, "Over half the people in my photo album are dead—either by getting shot, overdosing, or killing themselves. You always picture people you care about as invincible. And it's really weird to find out they're not. It's easy to get close to people here because we're all so entwined in each other's lives. We're not just numbers. We have faces and names and feelings."[30] Eleven students graduated from Sobriety High in 1994. All remain drug-free.

SMALLER SCHOOLS, SMALLER PROBLEMS

Next to the family, schools are the primary institutions in the lives of children. Much school violence is a result of overcrowding. Smaller schools allow the staff to know each student. In overcrowded schools, there are too many students in each class for teachers to take time to find out why one student missed class, did not turn in his or her homework, or failed an exam. If students see no one follows up with a phone call to their parents when these problems occur, the message is clear that cutting school and not doing lessons is okay.

Statistics show many kids who cut school eventually commit crimes. And the crimes escalate so that a misdemeanor such as truancy eventually becomes a felony such as armed robbery—which can quickly become murder when a kid has a gun. In addition, smaller schools give students a chance to get personal attention from their teachers, who can answer their questions individually and explain whatever they do not understand. Moreover, any problems between students can be stopped immediately, before they escalate into violence.

Deborah Prothrow-Stith, who pioneered violence prevention curriculums in schools, says the essence of violence prevention is that anger is normal. And handling anger is an important part of growing up. Fighting is only one way to deal with anger. Her curriculum also emphasizes conflict resolution, which teaches students skills to handle conflicts without violence. "What would happen if a fight started but everybody went the other way, and there was no crowd?" she asks her students. "It's an interesting question because we're trained to run toward a fight, and the crowd is so much a part of the fight."[31] Most of the time, students answer that there would not be a fight.

BUILDING CHARACTER AT SCHOOL

In Dayton, Ohio, 78 percent of kids at the Allen Classical Traditional Academy elementary school are in families that receive welfare. Behavior problems relating to the family were spilling over into school. In 1989, Allen started a character-building program. Each week, homeroom teachers introduce a new character trait, such as *responsibility* or *kindness*, and discuss it for five minutes. Throughout the day, teachers work the trait into their class lessons. If the word of the week is *honesty*, for example, the math teacher might give a student wrong change from a dollar and see how he or she reacts.

The Allen School has gone from fifth from the bottom in academic achievement in 1989 to second from the top in 1993. Its success has inspired a national character-building program called Stop, Think, Act, Review (STAR), now being taught to thousands of elementary school kids across the country.[32]

Newman Smith High School in Carrolton, Texas, inspired by the movie *Stand and Deliver*, decided to improve student performances in math. Talented but underachieving students were told they were expected to succeed in advanced math. In 1994, ninety students scored a 3 or better out of a possible 5 on the Advanced Placement Calculus Exam, which tests college-level ability.[33]

PARENT SHOCK AT BOWLING PARK ELEMENTARY SCHOOL

The sign on the building in the middle of the crime-ridden public-housing projects in Norfolk, Virginia, reads, BOWLING PARK ELEMENTARY: A CARING COMMUNITY. Principal Herman Clark cares not only about his students, but about their parents as well. He believes rescuing children requires rescuing whole families along with them. That is why every year he takes the parents on a field trip. But these are not your usual outings.

One time, parents went to Greensville Correctional Center in Jarratt, Virginia, where they saw the electric chair up close. Other times they have visited a men's prison in Chesapeake and a women's penal institution in Goochland and have taken a walk through Death Row at Mecklenburg Correctional Center. Principal Clark asks the inmates what led them to a life of crime. Most say their parents were not there for them when they were kids. There was nothing to do, so they fell into crime. The experience is frightening to parents and makes them realize that if they do not stay involved in their kids' lives, their kids will probably end up staying permanently at one of these field trip locations.

Every three years, the students go on a similar field trip. Before entering a prison, they are subjected to a shakedown body search for weapons or drugs, just like real prisoners. Returning from one prison visit, even the bullies were crying.[34]

THE CARING COMMUNITY REVOLUTION

Other "caring community schools" like Bowling Park Elementary are popping up all over the country. The idea is the school assumes responsibility for the foundations of learning—the emotional and social well-being of the child from birth to age twelve. Thus, anything that affects a child is the school's business, from nutrition to drug abuse prevention to health care and psychological counseling. Such schools become surrogate parents who increase the teachability of children who are at risk for trouble later on.

One program, which began in Missouri and spread to forty-seven states, hires "parent educators" who offer parenting skills to families, beginning in the seventh month of the mother's pregnancy. After the baby is born, teachers visit the family on a regular basis, eventually working with the toddler to teach numbers, colors, and the alphabet. Children whose parents are in the program get priority slots in caring community preschools associated with the program.[35]

COZI SCHOOLS

In 1992, Bowling Park was chosen as the first CoZi school, a model that combines the education programs of two Yale professors, James P. Comer and Edward Zigler. (CoZi is formed from the first two letters of the professors' names.) Comer, a psychiatrist, has helped convert 600 mostly inner-city schools to a cooperative management in which parents, teachers, and mental-health counselors jointly decide policy and focus on building close relationships with children. Zigler, a founder of Head Start, designed "The School of the 21st Century," a program operating on 400 campuses. It offers year-round all-day preschools, beginning at age three, as well as before-school, after-school, and vacation programs. Bowling Park combines the two professors' approaches, both of which focus on the success of the child.

As part of the CoZi school system at Bowling Park, staff members "adopt" a child, either a child whose parent has died or gone to prison, whose siblings are dealing or using drugs, or whose single mother neglects them. "We take these kids home with us for the weekend or out to eat or to get a haircut," says Principal Clark. "School has to be about more than reading, writing and arithmetic. These kids need so much—and sometimes what they really need is a good hug."[36]

PARENT INVOLVEMENT

The key to caring community schools is getting the parents involved. Many had never even walked their first graders to class. Parent aids visit parents at home and spur them to form committees and organize projects. Bowling Park now offers adult-education courses, exercise classes, a once-a-month Family Breakfast Club, where parents talk about children's books, and a "room moms" program that puts parents into the classroom to help teachers.

The other key to success of these schools is the staff's caring about both students and parents. When one mother's husband died, leaving her to raise six sons alone, parent technicians started a workshop on grief. A welfare mother who put her child in foster care found her self-confidence so improved by parenting classes that she took back her daughter and got a secretarial job.

But the lessons of Bowling Park are not just for schools attended by the poor. The concept of expanding school into a full-day, year-round experience is equally valuable to middle-class parents. Says Robert Watkins, the superintendent of schools in Independence, Missouri, "We have fine buildings. Why let them sit vacant fourteen hours a day and three months of the year? Now we can see a child with a speech impediment at age three and get started on remediation."[37]

COMMUNITY POLICING

Across the country, police forces are applying new strategies of conflict resolution to nip violence in the bud. Called *community policing*, the strategy means cops patrol the streets on foot rather than in squad cars and get to know the kids who live in the neighborhoods. They attempt to get rid of the sources of crime, such as open-air drug marts, rather than just arrest the perpetrators. Police officers are also encouraged to live in the neighborhoods they patrol. In Columbia, South Carolina, for example, police officers are offered low-interest loans without down payments to buy and rehabilitate inner-city houses.[38]

COPS

In New Orleans, Louisiana, just a few blocks from the Latin Quarter, is a street of trashed storefronts and bullet-riddled housing projects once called the most dangerous street in America. In the late 1980s, drug dealers claimed the neighborhood and turf wars and drive-by shootings ruled the streets. On the streets outside the St. Philip Social Service Center School, there were three or more killings each month, and preschoolers at the school learned to dive for the floor in "shooting drills" and stay there until teachers sounded the all clear.

In 1995, the city established a Community Oriented Policing Squad, called COPS for short. Headed by police lieutenant Edwin Compass III, COPS set up round-the-clock substations in vacant apartments. The forty-five police officers assigned to them work foot patrol, get to know the residents, get rid of street dealers, help pick up litter, and combat graffiti. They also provide counseling on child abuse, round up kids who play hooky, help kids with their homework, and give them treats when they get good grades.

At the same time, police are tougher in handling potential problem situations. "If we see somebody we don't know, we ask them what they're doing there," says Lieutenant Compass. "If the story doesn't check out, we arrest them for trespassing. Now we don't see as many drug dealers here."[39] By the end of 1995, killings in the neighborhood had dropped 74 percent.[40]

COMSTAT

In May 1994, then New York City Police Commissioner William Bratton designed a system called COMSTAT (short for *computer statistics*). COMSTAT consists of morning precinct meetings in which New York's seventy-six precinct commanders must account to the commissioner for crimes committed in their precincts. Each precinct was assigned a "war room" in which computer screens showed maps of areas where crimes occurred, diagramming patterns the same way former Oakland Raiders Coach John Madden diagrammed football plays.[41]

If the patterns showed increases in muggings along Manhattan's Ninth Avenue, for example, the police captain of the precinct would explain to the commissioner what his precinct was doing to arrest those responsible. Those precinct commanders who showed up without strategies to reduce crime were stripped of their commands.

New York City Mayor Rudolph Guiliani instructed the commissioner to use police to crack down on minor offenders, public drunks, potheads, people who urinate on the street, aggressive panhandlers, and graffiti scribblers. Thus was tested criminologists James Q. Wilson and George L. Kelling's broken windows theory, which postulates that minor violations create a disorderly environment that encourages more-serious crime. Therefore, it follows that stopping minor crimes will help reduce serious crimes. Sure enough, as arrests for small offenses skyrocketed, violent crime in New York's streets plummeted.[42]

PROMOTING POSITIVE ATTITUDES TOWARD POLICE

New York City has proved that police *can* and *do* make a difference in crime rates, which have fallen farther and faster there than anywhere else in the country. Total felonies in New York City dropped 27 percent between 1994 and 1996. Besides reducing crime rates, however, community policing has changed people's attitude about police—from a belief

Officer Russ Thurman of the East Palo Alto Police Department represents one of the success stories of community policing. Since the program's inception, he has seen a sharp decline in crime in his city.

they are useful only in catching criminals *after* they strike, to a trust that they can do something to stop crime from happening in the first place. Elisandra Beltran, twenty-seven, from one of the high-crime areas of New York, said, "It used to be that I was throwing myself on the floor with my son all the time because of the bullets flying through my window. But now I haven't seen a bullet hole in a year."[43]

JOB TRAINING PROGRAMS

Youth Employment Systems (YES), created in Los Angeles, helps young people who have been in serious trouble. Teenagers are paid real wages for doing real work, such as building affordable housing, renovating homes of elderly people, or reconstructing dilapidated houses to be sold at market value. When the job is finished, they have something they built with their own hands.

Members of the community-based policing team of the sheriff's department work with these kids. These officers believe kids who want to get out of the gang need something to replace that. A girl named Pea says, "Before I got into the program, my main goal was to marry a drug dealer, because I'd never have to work. My dream now is to do everything honestly. One of my friends who sells drugs had an argument with me about dealing drugs and making money. He said, 'I have all the money I ever dreamed of, lots of cars, and two homes. And I'm nineteen. But you have one thing I don't have. You can sleep at night.'"[44]

ON-THE-JOB CAREER COUNSELING

Besides doing job training, professionals in many communities are holding workshops for kids in different professional careers that require an advanced education. One such program was started by an African-American cardiologist, Dr. Donald Ware, in Los Angeles. He got the idea when the media said the television sitcom "The Cosby Show," about a prosperous black doctor and his wife, a lawyer, was unrealistic and that such black families did not actually exist. Dr. Ware set out to prove such black families do indeed exist. But Dr. Ware also set out to prove something much more difficult to prove: that black inner-city youths could indeed succeed in professional careers.

But he realized many of these kids did not have role models to show them how. So in 1995, Dr. Ware started "Youth Empowered for Survival," a program that teams up black students from South Los Angeles high schools with black professionals. His first career workshop targeted students with grade averages of A through C. They met with 100 professionals, from doctors and lawyers to celebrities such as James Worthy of the Lakers and actress Marla Gibbs.

In 1996, another workshop was held, this time including a live teleconference with retired general Colin Powell, followed by group discussions with professionals in fields ranging from law and medicine to mortuary science. The workshop was followed up with a series of field trips in which students visited professionals at work and participated in their specific career.

For example, the group of students who visited the medical center where Dr. Ware practices were invited to sit in on a cardiac procedure in which a tube is inserted into the patient's groin and through a vein into the heart to measure the pressure inside. "I felt good," said Kernel Stain, seventeen, after watching the procedure. She said she has always wanted to be a nurse or doctor and was inspired by her experience. Other student groups went to QUEST Records, composer Quincy Jones's music company, to learn about the entertainment industry. And still other groups flew with a helicopter pilot in the L.A. County Sheriff's department, or worked with elected city officials in downtown offices.

Another of Dr. Ware's goals is to open a camp where students who have at least a 3.0 grade average but score only moderately on college entrance exams can spend a week preparing to take the test. "We want to make that which is invisible visible," said Dr. Ware.[45] His career workshops and on-the-job field trips are doing just that.

A GARDEN OF HOPE

Of all the examples of help for kids who kill, perhaps the following stands out as proof that even the most at-risk kids can rise above an environment of crime and lead honest, productive, happy lives. In South Central Los Angeles, one of the most violent, dangerous neighborhoods in the country, a unique "victory garden" grew out of the 1992 racial riots. A group of forty students at Crenshaw High School, inspired by their biology teacher, decided to beautify the weedy quarter-acre plot behind the school's football field. Their goal was to create a community garden that would bring a sense of peace and life back to the neighborhood, while at the same time giving students hands-on science experience. Kids planted flowers, herbs, lettuce, collard greens, and other vegetables. A colorful mural soon appeared on the back wall, with a brown hand reaching toward a white one.

In the middle of the ghetto, an oasis began to bloom. The kids donated some of the produce to needy families in South Central, and sold the rest at local farmers' markets. They named their project "Food From the 'Hood." Spurred on by their success, the students decided to diversify. What could be a better accompaniment to vegetables than salad dressing? They created their own recipe, designed their own label, and called the brand "Straight Out the Garden." Local business leaders helped with the manufacturing and marketing. Soon the dressing was selling for $2.59 a bottle in twenty-three states. Students expected to earn $50,000 in profits by the end of 1995, which will go toward funding college scholarships.

More important than the money is the sense of accomplishment that has grown out of the garden. The students run all aspects of the business, from planting to public relations. Food From the 'Hood has received inquiries from across the country from people interested in duplicating their business plan, and they may franchise their logo to a group of New York kids who hope to sell applesauce. In addition to, and maybe as a result of, their success, ten of

After the riots of 1992, students in South Central Los Angeles created a community garden, not only as a science project but also as an attempt to "bring life back to one of the city's most battered neighborhoods." They called their project "Food From the 'Hood." Some of the money they raise from growing and selling vegetables goes into a college scholarship fund.

the fifteen seniors in Food From the 'Hood have been accepted at four-year colleges—an incredible record for an inner-city public school. Members also have set up a mentor system and a SAT preparatory program.[46]

Food From the 'Hood shows that from anything—even racial riots—amazing things can grow. And from poverty, abuse, and a lack of family love and values, successful, happy, crime-free kids can grow.

REMEMBERING KEVIN

Sixteen-year-old Kevin Grant grew up on the tough streets of Brooklyn, New York. Many of his friends spent their after-school hours hanging out with gangs, dealing drugs, mugging, and killing. Kevin managed to stay out of a gang. But teen violence troubled him deeply. So during his junior year in high school, in 1990, he joined a New York City internship program at the Educational Video Center (EVC). His group chose teen crime as their video project. Their film, titled *Youth Crime: Who's to Blame?*, features Kevin and other EVC interns talking to teen criminals, crime victims, and concerned New Yorkers.

The series of interviews presents an honest, chilling account of teen crime in the city and was so well regarded that it was shown in classrooms around New York. Praise for the video poured in from educators and young people alike. But Kevin never heard one word of the praise. On June 14, about two weeks after he finished the tape, and before it was seen in the classrooms, he was walking home when he saw two kids fighting over a skateboard. When Kevin tried to settle the fight peaceably, one of the kids pulled out a gun and shot him, killing him instantly.

Within months of Kevin's death, his friends at EVC began another video about teen violence and dedicated it to Kevin. Included in the film is a reading from an essay

Kevin wrote on teen crime: "Things are getting worse in this generation. The attitude of kids . . . is they do not seem to care what happens to them, and in their community this is 'cool.' Many more kids are being shot by other kids their age, and they have no pity. To kids today, going to jail is something they get praised for by their friends.

"Too many young children are turning to crime for fun. . . . Every crime you can think of, there are kids from the age of ten to fifteen who can master it. It is said that children are the future. If most of the children are juvenile delinquents, what is the future going to be like?"[47]

Most kids do not grow up to be violent. So America must take action to help the kids who *are* on the road to violence and murder. More programs need to be developed to help these kids believe their lives can be productive and worthwhile without resorting to crime and murder, programs like Mad Dads, Big Brothers, the CoZi caring community schools, and programs that offer support to kids *after* they get out of juvenile facilities, so they have help to keep them from going back to a life of crime.

That is the real answer to the question, What can we do about kids who kill? The bottom line is kids will continue to kill unless "the entire village" gets involved in making America safe.

SOURCE NOTES

CHAPTER ONE

1. Nancy R. Gibbs, "Murder in Miniature," *Time* (September 19, 1994), 56.

2. Ibid., 57.

3. Ibid., 58.

4. Ibid.

5. Ibid.

6. Julie Grace, "There Are No Children Here," *Time* (September 12, 1994). Transmitted through Prodigy On-Line Services.

7. Gibbs, "Murder in Miniature," 59.

8. Howard N. Snyder and Melissa Sickmund, U.S. Department of Justice, "Report of the Office of Juvenile Justice and Delinquency Prevention," Special Report, August 1995, 48.

9. Ted Gest and Victoria Pope, "Rising Juvenile Crime," *U.S. News & World Report* (March 25, 1996), 29.

10. Steven Manning, "A National Emergency," *Scholastic Update* (April 5, 1991), 2.

11. Gest and Pope, "Rising Juvenile Crime," 29.

12. Ibid., 32.

13. Richard A. Serrano and David G. Savage, "Colorado Tries a

Kick in the Pants to Fight Teen Crime," *Los Angeles Times* (July 10, 1996), Section A-10.

14. Gest and Pope, "Rising Juvenile Crime," 36.

15. Richard Lacayo, "When Kids Go Bad," *Time* (September 19, 1994), 61.

16. Michele Weiner-Davis, "The Lost Boys," *Ladies Home Journal* (January 1995), 85.

17. Gest and Pope, "Rising Juvenile Crime," 30.

18. Ibid., 32.

19. Ibid., 30.

20. Serrano and Savage, "Colorado Tries a Kick in the Pants."

21. Lacayo, "When Kids Go Bad," 63.

22. Fox Butterfield, "Grim Forecast Is Offered on Rising Juvenile Crime," *New York Times* (September 8, 1995), Section A-1.

23. Catherine Tatge and Dominique Lasseur, "What Can We Do About Violence?" Narrated by Bill Moyers, PBS Special, January 9, 1995 (hereafter cited as Moyers, PBS Special).

24. Weiner-Davis, "The Lost Boys," 78.

25. Ibid.

26. *Diagnostic & Statistical Manual of Mental Disorders*, 4th ed. (Washington, D.C.: American Psychiatric Association, 1994), 85–91.

27. Weiner-Davis, "The Lost Boys," 78.

28. Marsha Renee Conrad, "Youth Held for Killing After Bragging to Friends," *Jet* (December 17, 1981), 15.

29. Larry Garrison, "Kids Who Kill," *Oui* (December 1983), 32–37.

30. Butterfield, "Grim Forecast Is Offered."

31. Ibid.

32. Bettijane Levine, "A New Wave of Mayhem," *Los Angeles Times* (September 6, 1995), Section E-1.

33. Lacayo, "When Kids Go Bad," 62.

34. Serrano and Savage, "Colorado Tries a Kick in the Pants."

35. Frank B. Williams, "11-Year-Old Girl Slain on Porch in Drive-By Shooting," *Los Angeles Times* (October 28, 1995), Section B-1.

36. Lacayo, "When Kids Go Bad," 61.

37. Bill Moyers, PBS Special.

38. Ibid.

39. Ibid.

40. Gibbs, "Murder in Miniature," 56.

CHAPTER TWO

1. Nancy Traver, "Children Without Pity," *Time* (October 26, 1992), 46.

2. Weiner-Davis, "The Lost Boys," 85.

3. Travers, "Children Without Pity," 51.

4. Ibid.

5. Ibid.

6. Serrano and Savage, "Colorado Tries a Kick in the Pants."

7. Ibid.

8. Snyder and Sickmund, U.S. Department of Justice Special Report, 91.

9. Moyers, PBS Special.

10. Charles Molony Condon, "Clinton's Cocaine Babies," *Policy Review*, The Heritage Foundation (1995), 1. Transmitted through America Online.

11. Katherine Greider, "Crack Babies," *Mother Jones* (July–August, 1995), 55.

12. Ibid., 56.

13. Bettijane Levine, "A New Wave of Mayhem," *Los Angeles Times* (September 6, 1995), Section E-4.

14. Moyers, PBS Special.

15. Ibid.

16. Snyder and Sickmund, U.S. Department of Justice Special Report, 1–11.

17. Ibid.

18. Moyers, PBS Special.

19. Levine, "A New Wave of Mayhem."

20. Lawrence Kazmin, "Judge Finds Youth Guilty of Murder in Russian Roulette," *Los Angeles Times* (August 31, 1989), Section B-8.

21. Ronald Henkoff, "Kids Are Killing, Dying, Bleeding," *Fortune* (August 10, 1992), 67.

22. Richard Brellis, "Teenager Charged in Slayings," *New York Times* (December 29, 1986), Section A-14.

23. Leslie Fraust, "A National Emergency," *Scholastic Update* (April 5, 1991), 8.

24. Associated Press, "Man Convicted of Violating Student's Civil Rights in Riot," *Daily Nexus* (February 11, 1997). Transmitted through America Online.

25. Gordon Witkin and Jeannye Thornton, "Pride and Prejudice," *U.S. News & World Report* (July 15/July 22, 1996), 74.

26. Ibid.

27. David Van Biema, "When White Makes Right," *Time* (August 9, 1993), 41.

28. Ibid.

29. Fraust, "A National Emergency," 6.

30. Ibid., 7.

31. Ibid.

32. Ibid.

33. Moyers, PBS Special.

34. Michael Marriott, "A Gangster Wake-Up Call," *Newsweek* (April 10, 1995), 74. "Shots Silence Angry Voice" *New York Times* (September 16, 1996), Section A-17.

35. Christopher John Farley, "First Tupac. Now Biggie. Has Gangsta Rap Gone Too Far?" *Time* (March 24, 1997). Transmitted through America Online.

36. Kevin Chappell, "Gangsta Rap and Raunchy Lyrics Raise National Debate," *Ebony* (September 1995), 26.

37. Farley, "First Tupac, Now Biggie."

38. Ibid.

39. Ibid.

40. James Q. Wilson, *Vital Speeches* (April 1, 1995), 373–377.

41. Henkoff, "Kids Are Killing, Dying, Bleeding," 63.

CHAPTER THREE

1. Ann W. O'Neill, "Menendezes Are Found Guilty of Killing Parents," *Los Angeles Times* (March 21, 1996), Section A-23.

2. Alan Abrahamson and Ann W. O'Neill, "New Strategy Pays Off for Prosecutors," *Los Angeles Times* (March 21, 1996), Section A-24.

3. O'Neill, "Menendezes Are Found Guilty."

4. Ann W. O'Neill, "Abuse Excuse Under Attack," *Los Angeles Times* (February 9, 1996), Section B-1.

5. Ibid.

6. Ibid.

7. Ibid.

8. O'Neill, "Menendezes Are Found Guilty."

9. Ann W. O'Neill and Nicholas Riccardi, "Menendez Brothers Sentenced to Life for Killing Parents," *Los Angeles Times* (April 18, 1996), Section A-1.

10. Gest and Pope, "Rising Juvenile Crime," 36.

11. Henkoff, "Kids Are Killing, Dying, Bleeding," 64.

12. Susan Howlett, "Days of Rage," *Los Angeles Times* (March 12, 1996), Section E-1.

13. John Dawson and Patrick A. Langan, "Murder in Families," Bureau of Statistics Special Report, July 1994, 1–4.

14. Howlett, "Days of Rage."

15. Efrain Hernandez, Jr., "Boy Said He Wanted to Shoot Someone, Two Friends Say," *Los Angeles Times* (August 18, 1996), Section B-1.

16. Judith Abrams, "Defender of the Indefensible," *Los Angeles Times* (June 7, 1989), Section E-1.

17. Dina Kleiman, "Murder in Long Island," *New York Times Magazine* (September 14, 1986), 52.

18. Ibid.

19. Snyder and Sickmund, U.S. Department of Justice Special Report, 42.

20. Ibid.

21. Ibid.

22. Ibid.

23. "Young Gets Life: Killed His Brother with a Bat," *Los Angeles Times* (December 12, 1989), Section A-25.

24. Joshua Hammer, "Driven by His Long-Buried Rage," *People Weekly* (November 18, 1985), 127–130.

25. Ibid.

26. Moyers, PBS Special.

CHAPTER FOUR

1. Weiner-Davis, "The Lost Boys," 85.

2. Ibid.

3. Ibid.

4. Ibid., 78.

5. Ben Dobbin, "Boy's Death Devastates Town," *Los Angeles Times* (April 3, 1994), Section A-1.

6. Times Wire Services, "Boy 14, Sentenced to 9 Years in Prison for Killing Child," *Los Angeles Times* (November 8, 1994), Section A-28.

7. Inset, "Sixteen-Year-Old Boy Charged As Adult in Murder of Boy Over a Quarter," *Jet* (August 21, 1995), 37.

8. Josef F. Sheley, Zina T. McGee, and James D. Wright, "Weapon-Related Victimization in Selected Inner-City High School Samples," National Institute of Justice Report, February 1995, 1–5.

9. Ibid.

10. Ibid.

11. James Gerstenzang, "Clinton Praises School Uniform Pacesetter," *Los Angeles Times* (February 25, 1996), Section A-15.

12. Susan Pack, "A Young Murderer Recalls the Day He Said: 'Daddy, I Killed Someone,'" *Long Beach Press-Telegram* (November 10, 1996), Section K-10.

13. Ibid.

14. Ibid.

15. Ibid.

16. Kim Murphy, "Teen Is Held in Deadly School Shootings," *Los Angeles Times* (February 3, 1996), Section A-1.

17. Ibid.

18. Ibid.

19. Insert/Nation, "It Was Monday," *Time* (February 12, 1979), 25.

20. Ibid.

21. John L. Mitchell and Amy Pyle, "Shootings Shatter Program for Safety at Dorsey High," *Los Angeles Times* (February 6, 1996), Section A-16.

22. Ibid.

23. Josef F. Sheley et al., "Weapon-Related Victimization," 1–5.

24. Ibid.

25. Ibid.

26. Gerstenzang, "Clinton Praises School Uniform Pacesetter."

27. James Earl Hardy, "Gang Warfare," *Scholastic Update* (April 5, 1991), 6.

28. Barbara Allen-Hagen, Melissa Sickmund, and Howard N. Snyder, "Juveniles and Violence: Juvenile Offending and Victimization," Office of Juvenile Justice and Delinquency Prevention, Fact Sheet 19, November 1994, 2.

29. Jodi Wilgoren, "New Anti-Gang Proposal Targets Middle Schools," *Los Angeles Times* (September 20, 1996), Section B-1.

30. Jeff Leeds and Eric Lichtblau, "Suspects Arrested in Drive-By Slaying of Three," *Los Angeles Times* (January 28, 1996), Section B-1.

31. Moyers, PBS Special.

32. Wilgoren, "New Anti-Gang Proposal."

33. Hardy, "Gang Warfare," 6.

34. James Willwerth, "Lessons Learned on Death Row," *Time* (September 23, 1996). Transmitted through America Online.

35. Ibid.

36. Ibid.

37. Hardy, "Gang Warfare," 6.

38. David Gelman, "Going Wilding in the City," *Newsweek* (May 8, 1989), 65.

39. Nancy Gibbs, "Wilding in the Night," *Time* (May 8, 1989), 20–21.

40. Ibid.

CHAPTER FIVE

1. Leslie Fraust, "What Kind of Justice?", *Scholastic Update* (April 5, 1991), 10.

2. Lacayo, "When Kids Go Bad," 61.

3. Ibid.

4. Leah Eskin, "Punishment or Reform? Juvenile Justice in U.S. History," *Scholastic Update* (April 5, 1991), 18–19.

5. Ibid., 18.

6. Ibid.

7. Ibid.

8. Ibid., 18–19.

9. Ibid., 19.

10. Ibid.

11. Lacayo, "When Kids Go Bad," 61.

12. Moyers, PBS Special.

13. Lacayo, "When Kids Go Bad," 61.

14. Moyers, PBS Special.

15. Lacayo, "When Kids Go Bad," 59–61.

16. Phil Sudo, "What Kind of Justice?" *Scholastic Update*, April 5, 1991, 11.

17. Levine, "A New Wave of Mayhem."

18. Moyers, PBS Special.

19. Lacayo, "When Kids Go Bad," 60.

20. Tony Perry, "Killer, Now 15, Sentenced to Prison," *Los Angeles Times* (February 9, 1996), Section B-1.

21. Ibid.

22. Lacayo, "When Kids Go Bad," 62.

23. Ibid.

24. Ibid.

25. Gest and Pope, "Rising Juvenile Crime," 36.

26. Ibid.

27. Moyers, PBS Special.

28. Mary Lou Loper, "Full Court Press," *Los Angeles Times* (September 22, 1996), Section E-1.

29. Ibid.

30. Moyers, PBS Special.

31. Fraust, "What Kind of Justice?", 12.

32. Moyers, PBS Special.

33. Fraust, "What Kind of Justice?", 13.

34. Ibid.

35. Philip Brasfield, "It Most Definitely Resembles a Crucifixion," *National Catholic Reporter* (November 8, 1985), 11–13.

36. U.S. Department of Justice, Office of Juvenile Justice, "Imposition of Death Penalty for Juvenile Crimes Is Rare," Special Report, 178.

37. Ibid.

38. Leslie Fraust, "The Ultimate Price," *Scholastic Update* (April 5, 1991), 13.

39. James Q. Wilson, *Vital Speeches* (April 1, 1995), 373–377.

40. Ibid.

41. U.S. Department of Justice, Office of Juvenile Justice and Delinquency Prevention, "Interview with Judge David B. Mitchell," *Juvenile Justice* (spring/summer 1993), 8.

CHAPTER SIX

1. Michael Krikorian, "Rescued from A Dark Path," *Los Angeles Times* (February 18, 1996), Section B-1.

2. Ibid.

3. Richard Lacayo, "Lock 'Em Up," *Time* (February 7, 1994). Transmitted through Prodigy On-Line.

4. Sharon Stewart, "Finding Solutions," *Long Beach Press Telegram* (November 10, 1996), Section K-9.

5. Ibid.

6. Ibid.

7. Jonathan Alter, "Intervene Earlier and More Often," *Newsweek* (May 29, 1995), 20.

8. Stewart, "Finding Solutions."

9. Alter, "Intervene Earlier and More Often," 20.

10. Carla Hall, "Mentor Makes a Mark in a 12-Year-Old's Life," *Los Angeles Times* (November 17, 1996), Section B1–4.

11. Gordon Witkin, "Colorado Has a New Brand of Tough Love," *U.S. News & World Report* (March 25, 1996), 38–39.

12. Serrano and Savage, "Colorado Tries a Kick in the Pants."

13. Krikorian, "Rescued from a Dark Path."

14. Serrano and Savage, "Colorado Tries a Kick in the Pants."

15. Lauren Tarshis, "Life on the Inside," *Scholastic Update* (April 5, 1991), 16.

16. Ibid., 16–17.

17. Moyers, PBS Special.

18. Serrano and Savage, "Colorado Tries a Kick in the Pants."

19. Fraust, "The Ultimate Price," 12.

20. Jill Smolowe, "Parenting on Trial," *Time* (May 20, 1996), 50.

21. Ibid.

22. Ibid.

23. Moyers, PBS Special.

24. Jonathan Alter, "Get the Community Involved," *Newsweek* (May 29, 1995), 24.

25. Bob Pool, "Black, Latino Men Join Fight Against Drug Violence," *Los Angeles Times* (October 20, 1996), Section B-1.

26. Alter, "Get the Community Involved," 24.

27. Moyers, PBS Special.

28. Ibid.

29. Ibid.

30. Ibid.

31. Moyers, PBS Special.

32. Jonathan Alter, "Build a Sense of Character," *Newsweek* (May 29, 1995), 21.

33. Jonathan Alter, "Set High Standards," *Newsweek* (May 29, 1995), 24.

34. Margot Hornblower, "It Takes a School," *Time* (June 3, 1996), 36.

35. Ibid., 36.

36. Ibid., 37.

37. Ibid., 38.

38. Alter, "Get the Community Involved," 24.

39. Ibid., 51.

40. Ibid.

41. Eric Pooley, "One Good Apple," *Time* (January 15, 1996), 54.

42. Ibid., 56.

43. Ibid.

44. Michael Krikorian, "Partners in Crime," *Los Angeles Times* (March 7, 1996), Section B-2.

45. Mark Becker, "Students Say YES To Success," *Los Angeles Times* (March 6, 1996), Section B-2.

46. Lester Sloan, "Planting Seeds, Harvesting Scholarships," *Newsweek* (May 29, 1995), 29.

47. Lauren Tarshis, "A Shot that Echoed," *Scholastic Update* (April 5, 1991), 20–21.

INDEX